K-POP SECRET LOVE

K-POP SECRET LOVE

My Romance with a K-pop Idol

Sandy N. Olson

K-pop Secret Love is work of fiction. Names, characters, places and incidents are the products of the author's imagination or are used fictitiously. Any resemblance to actual events, locales, or persons living or dead is entirely coincidental.

Copyright © 2019 by Sandy N. Olson

All rights reserved. The moral rights of the author have been asserted. No part of this book may be reproduced or used in any manner without written permission of the copyright owner except for the use of quotations in a book review.

Published in the United States of America by Sunlight4us Books. www.sunlight4usbooks.com

Paperback ISBN 978-1-7347915-0-1
eBook ISBN 978-1-7347915-1-8

1 2 3 4 5 6 7 8 9 10
First Edition published in January 2021

TABLE OF CONTENTS

1. MY JOB WITH A K-POP BAND 1
2. US TOUR 29
3. CHICAGO, DALLAS AND NEW YORK 51
4. AN INVITATION 65
5. PARIS 71
6. MONET'S GARDENS 85
7. INTRODUCTIONS 95
8. DEEPER DISCUSSIONS 113
9. BACK TO WORK 133
10. THANKSGIVING IN CALIFORNIA 161
11. SURPRISES 169
12. THE UNEXPECTED 187
13. MARA'S ESCAPE 203
14. REALIZATION 211
15. THE FUTURE 221

My Job with a K-pop Band

My name is Mara Jansen. I want to share a beautiful love story with you – one that I never dreamed would happen to me.

♥

Like most of my single friends, at twenty-five I was beginning to wonder if I would ever meet someone I could really love and admire, long term. Not that I'm in any hurry to marry, just tired of being disillusioned. Maybe I'm too particular about the qualities I'm looking for.

My cousin and best friend, Bree, is a perfect source of encouragement, "Mara, you just haven't met him yet. You're extraordinary: smart, talented, and beautiful. Plus, you have a gift – you can communicate graciously with *the* toughest people and experience zero stress. That face of yours will always open doors. You can navigate to any level in this life! Don't settle for some guy who isn't worthy of you."

My response is always, "Thanks, Bree, but I'm beginning to wonder if that guy even exists. Where is he? If I ever find him, you'll be my first text."

What I couldn't know then? I'll be halfway around the world when I meet that man and I'll feel sparks the instant I shake his hand. But, if he responds to me, it could threaten my career, even my life…and his. If I knew then a hint of what I know now, I guess I'd be asking - Could such a romance last?

Sandy N. Olson

♥

I had an excellent professional reputation when my Los Angeles public relations firm recommended me for a new PR job. The assignment was to manage publicity for a South Korean boy band during the US leg of their world tour.

The six-member group was known in South Korea as the Brave Lions. But that name had been shortened to BL6 when they landed their first singles on US charts last year.

The handsome members were all extremely talented, in their 20s, and had worked together for four years. They were rising stars in K-pop (Korean pop music), a phenomenon the US market didn't know very much about. They'd built a huge social media presence. Now, BL6 was gaining global recognition and preparing for their second world tour. With this tour, they want to become America's K-pop leaders.

Beyond my work on two chart-topping national tours – one that took a YouTuber mainstream – I had an added qualification as the firm's first choice. I had learned basic Korean when Bree moved to Seoul on a temporary consulting assignment.

She'd excelled in international business while earning her MBA. Now Bree was working her way around the world.

Her impressive command of the beautiful Korean language got me interested enough to take lessons. But by the time I earned the BL6 tour – a feat in our friendly but competitive

PR office – Bree had accepted work with a firm that would bring her back to the US. We joked that she'd toss me her dictionary as our planes crossed paths.

I loved the idea of working internationally. Bree was quick to remind me, my "negotiating grace" could serve me well with Seoul's music industry players. I rarely felt overwhelmed by my work, I enjoyed it. It's personal relationships that cause me stress, especially romantic ones.

Managing BL6 was the increasingly influential Korean entertainment company, BestStars. They offered our firm the consulting contract and me the title, 'Assistant Manager of US Publicity.' For the duration of the North American tour – about a month with a few weeks of lead time – my job was to generate publicity for each concert, building ticket sales with smart media bookings and articles.

I'd liaise between BestStars management and online publications, print editors, influencers, radio and TV producers to book appearances. Packaging exclusive material for channels to share was key, with a K-pop crash course tailored to TV show hosts.

Also, I'd be communicating with arena managers about what the group and support crew traveling with them might need available pre-show for each concert. In the meantime, a BestStars employee would manage social media - Twitter, Facebook, VLIVE, Instagram, and others.

Last year's first BL6 tour of the US was limited in scope but had surprising success. Recently, the group's latest releases had been blowing up worldwide. Fans were finding and falling in love with the music – the band members, too. So, BL6 was better-known and more saleable now.

They had made substantial gains in social media: videos, constant in-house photo shoots, even their own reality series, all created by BestStars. In my business that's called "owned media." It's all the group or artist's content for social channels, press releases, group websites and blogs.

What I bring is the "earned media" – influencers, mainstream media, and sharable content from traditional TV, streaming, print and radio, plus the blog and destination site coverage every group needs if they want chart-topping superstar status.

That balance between earned and owned media is about split-second timing. So, integrating with a group's social media company is a key part of amplifying each appearance's impact. Getting news to fans on shared platforms before the general public knows it's happening matters – just like boosting "shares" during and after it's run.

In the months before the group was to arrive in LA for their first concert, June 22nd, I completed an interview in the US with a BestStars' representative. Next came video conferences with the band's managers in Seoul.

Company culture was imperative to BestStars. I learned they did all owned media production in-house, plus most of their shared media management. For me, their idea of keeping a full-time social media department on staff was innovative and, likely, a lucrative move.

To get me up to speed, BestStars decided I should meet the band and executives ASAP. So, on May 10th, I flew to Seoul, excited about the opportunity to work from South Korea until the start of the tour.

I arrived late in the evening after a very long flight. The next morning, I had a meeting with BL6 and their three managers. The top manager, Choi Hyun-Tae, is a very personable man with whom I had interviewed in LA.

Joining the meeting would be two other managers. One was the head of security and the other was BestStars' head publicist – my supervisor for this assignment. These managers always traveled with the band, as I would for the US segment.

By the way, Koreans use their family name first, then their given name follows. So, Choi is the family name for the BL6 lead manager. He was probably in his early 30s. I referred to him as Manager Choi, in keeping with cultural tradition.

The band included the leader, Ki, whom I had read is very bright and is fluent in English. His family name is Lee and his given name is Ki-Yoon. The other members are known as Bin, Sunny, Kwon, Val and JJ. They are learning English and can understand it more easily than speak it.

As soon as I knew the company wanted me for this gig, I began reviewing their portfolio – videos of BL6 songs, humorous episodes of their reality shows, interviews, etc. They were likable and impressively kind toward each other.

From the videos, I already had a favorite (or "bias" as fans say), Ki, the group leader. I liked his thoughtfulness, sense of humor, and patience with the other members. He seems very caring – a hallmark in many of the best artists I'd seen.

For the morning meeting after my flight, the band members and their managers were already seated and chatting when I arrived at the spacious conference room. I wasn't late, instead, they were early.

As soon as I walked through the open door, all nine men stood and bowed to me as they said, "Good Morning," in English. They were all smiling. I felt humbled and excited to receive such a gracious greeting.

I nodded to them, formally, in return and said in Korean, "Thank you, gentlemen, that is a lovely welcome. It is my honor to be chosen to work with you."

Each of the band members was even more handsome in person compared to the videos I had reviewed.

Their senior manager, Choi Huyn-Tae, said, "Ms. Jansen, welcome to the group. As you know, in professional South

K-pop Secret Love

Korean custom, we would not normally address a business associate by his or her name. But we're a little more informal here since we work in international entertainment. Because you are an American and asked me during our interview to address you by name, we will follow your culture in this respect."

Dear Reader, Although we continued speaking in Korean, I will use English in sharing my story with you.

I answered, "Thank you, Manager Choi. Gentlemen, if you feel comfortable doing so, please call me by my given name, Mara."

Manager Choi continued, "Thank you. As you have met the other managers during the video conference calls, I'll let the BL6 members introduce themselves."

I nodded and shook hands first with each of the managers and we exchanged polite comments. Then, I took a step toward Ki, nodded and offered my hand to shake his. This is in keeping with what I'd learned was acceptable of Western businesspeople interacting with Korean custom.

He took my hand, warmly smiled at me and said, "I'm Ki, the leader of the group. We're happy to have you here to help us."

I smiled in return, looking up at his remarkable face. As soon as our hands touched, I felt something - an emotional reaction, a spark - and became unexpectedly nervous.

I'm a businesswoman who has dealt with handsome male celebrities before. My reaction to meeting Ki was surprising. But I kept that surprise well-hidden.

I had to be ideally balanced between friendly and formal in my interactions with the whole group. I knew that my job depended on my ability to do so. My contract with BestStars even included a clause stating that employees and consultants could not date BL6 members.

I moved along the line of these six extraordinary men; each greeted me warmly, especially Val, who seemed very sweet and sensitive.

Without any sign of facial hair, the members looked younger than their ages. They're all taller than my five-foot, six-inches, each friendly and charming, particularly Ki, who was the tallest and oldest – twenty-five at the time (my age). JJ was the youngest at twenty.

Manager Choi said, "Ms. Jansen, I understand that you have a presentation for us regarding US media appearances, digital and print platforms for which the boys might be ideal. As you are aware, we'd like to do the LA publicity before the first concert while tickets are on sale. You can start that presentation now if you're ready."

"Thank you, Manager Choi. Gentlemen, in the brief I'll give you now, each of you will find an outline of select national and local TV, online and print media along with key LA-based influencers and bloggers. This select earned-media is grouped by city for the full tour and paired to audience demographics for your VLIVE, Facebook and additional social channels with some reach into wider audiences on certain national shows.

"Manager Choi, you'll find market share and audience data for each is included. Also, there are conservative projections for shared media. These numbers will be met using the combined reach of social media from each outlet.

"Gentlemen, my plan is to arrange shoots, tour coverage, interviews and appearances that keep your schedules manageable but capitalize on the generous promotional time built into this US leg of the tour. This morning, we'll do an overview of these materials. I'll play clips of the LA-based shows and Influencer feeds to familiarize you with the hosts and their programming tone. You will each receive a link following this meeting so you can review them further and ask me any other questions that arise.

"Today I would like to learn which of the shows and feeds you like most. I'll begin work to confirm bookings and use the social team's owned content to shape pitches and press releases. I'm here to support you on this tour and will bring all my networks and creativity to make your US dates a major success. I've reviewed your outstanding body of work and very much admire your professionalism."

The members responded with smiles and nods, some saying, "Thank you."

We had a productive discussion. The team had good questions about each of the clips and decided which appearances they preferred. We had several weeks before we would all head to LA. The morning's discussion lasted about an hour and we scheduled our next meeting for Chicago, Dallas and New York within three days.

I then headed to my new, temporary office in the building and began efforts to book the initial media support. Coordinating with their social and streaming team was easy since we were all in the same space.

In a step beyond other management companies and unlike my US clients, BestStars had recently developed their own internal PR/Social Media reporting software. It did a lot of the tracking, compiling and data extrapolation for me. It was only in beta but, for true PR workaholics like me, what fun breaking it in!

That afternoon, San-A, the warm and very polished director of the BestStars social team, walked me over to the IT department where my company phone was assigned. She gave me a full tutorial on their proprietary management software. It was unlike anything I'd ever seen a music client do – even among the big record labels.

Not only was I able to do all the tracking and compiling I'd usually filter through my firm and then, into a daily BestStars report, I could also get time-sensitive images from the road back here to San-A in Seoul more securely than if I were trying to text them from my phone or a hackable email account using airport wifi. Another innovation that upped my admiration for BestStars.

It seemed they operating well beyond most integrated marketing strategies and I felt even more fortunate to be on this assignment by the end of Day One.

The time difference between Seoul and LA required that most calls and Zooms with US journalists or producers be done during afternoons and evenings. At first, I thought this might give me some solo time in the office, after hours. But I soon learned that a few of us were working on international time and that South Koreans are highly accustomed to ten-hour days.

BL6 and the managers were happy with my first week's work. We were starting later than usual in booking the group on more popular shows. But I used my network to get them featured on most programs they'd wanted, always taking care not to overtax vital professional relationships. Once booked, I negotiated key questions and topics the hosts would cover.

Everyone in the group of managers and idols (the South Korean term for K-pop singers) was friendly toward me – except Ki. After our first meeting, he seemed distant. But I assumed it was because he had a lot on his mind.

During each meeting, we all shared easy laughter over something one or two of the group would say, even things I said once I allowed my sense of humor to come through. I couldn't think of anything that I had said or done to have offended Ki.

In the second week of my employment, *two important events occurred.*

The first was that the company publicist, my supervisor, revealed to Manager Choi that he had been coping with a painful illness and had been diagnosed with a condition that required bed rest to avert hospitalization. He had been hiding how bad his health was until now and was very sorry that he couldn't continue his job heading into the tour's launch.

Because he had been tracking my work and observing my conversations with US media personnel, he recommended to Manager Choi that I take full charge of the US phase of the tour. He believed I could handle it effectively.

I felt sad that he'd become ill. But I couldn't deny the value of the promotion. Manager Choi spoke with my firm in LA and, *bam,* I was a manager instead of an assistant, with more freedom and a better salary.

The second important event occurred midway through week two at the end of a mid-morning meeting. As the managers and band members left the room, Ki lingered to ask me privately if I would like to go to a park nearby for a business lunch.

He clarified, "I'd like to ask a few more questions about the tour."

Surprised and pleased, I said, "I would love to."

He then phoned a café to prepare sandwiches and tea for us to pick up on our way.

It was a beautiful sunny day with trees blossoming and petals blowing in the breeze along each street. We walked to the park, a couple blocks away, stopping off for our take-out lunch.

Ki was a well-known celebrity in South Korea but no one bothered him for an autograph or to take his picture. Yet, I saw people all around us noticing him. To help hide his features, he was wearing sunglasses and a wide-rimmed bucket hat to cover his hair and forehead. I asked him about people looking but saying nothing.

He said, "Koreans are too polite to bother me but tourists might."

As we walked, he asked, "Have you seen much of Seoul since arriving?"

"I haven't because of the work."

"Well, I'm glad you could come with me today because this park is quite lovely."

As we arrived, it was immediately relaxing to see the rolling hills of green grass, beautiful trees and manicured shrubs amid the city. We found an empty bench and talked as we ate, while sipping tea.

Ki first asked a few questions about the LA publicity, then posed questions about me - how I got into my career, did I have siblings, and how long had I lived in LA. Although he had my resume and knew some basics about me, his questions went beyond that.

I said, "I chose to work in the area of publicity because I like the idea of working with celebrities and recognize that it's a difficult life to lead, always being in the public eye. I wanted to make their lives easier by helping with their careers and shielding them in whatever ways I could."

He smiled, "I especially appreciate that you recognize how celebrity life can be difficult. I struggle with it. I love writing songs and rapping, I love that I'm able to follow my dream, I even love being on stage; but there's a side of me that misses leading a normal life. I'm not enough of an extrovert that I flow with it easily. But I still want it. I want BL6 to be the best we can be."

I liked how open Ki was with me. I answered, "I greatly admire what you're doing. I couldn't do it. I couldn't be in the spotlight as you are. After this world tour, BL6's popularity will explode with all the positive publicity as you cross the US and Europe."

Regarding his questions about where I grew up and siblings, I shared, "I grew up in a little village not far from New York City where my parents owned a grocery store and were very well-liked by the people in our community.

"I have an older brother who is a good friend. He's now become a home contractor, married with two children. Because I went to college at UCLA, I left home at age eighteen and worked summers at the company where I'm still a consultant."

During this conversation, we had started by speaking Korean, but after a while Ki suggested we speak English so he could practice for the tour.

I was impressed with him. Not only did he ask good questions, but he also listened carefully to each of my answers. And, in most cases, asked a follow-up. I'd noticed that few men in business ask follow-ups, really few men in general.

Plus, he shared some of his background, "I grew up in a city a few miles from Seoul. I have a younger sister. My parents wanted me to go to college and be a businessman like my dad. They were against my being in the music business; in my teens, I kept my songwriting and rapping a secret from them.

"I wasn't an obedient son when I was a teen, I joined BestStars without telling my parents. Back then, they were very disappointed in me. It took a long time of playing to small venues around Seoul before BL6 began developing a fanbase. After those difficult years, I hope that now my parents feel somewhat proud of me." He said this with a bit of sadness in his eyes.

"I appreciate you sharing your background and feelings. I'm sorry you went through that period of difficulty and am sure your parents *do* feel proud of all that you're accomplishing."

As we were talking, an hour flew by. We continued talking on the way back to the BestStars' building. I felt very comfortable with Ki and he seemed to feel the same with me. I still wondered why he had been so distant from me during the first week; and now, it seemed he had gone in the opposite direction - friendly and kind.

Before we parted, Ki thanked me for going to the park with him and I thanked him for inviting me. Then, we returned to our offices. I hoped we would have another chance to spend time together soon. I felt intrigued by this intelligent, handsome man.

During the next week, I refined and finalized media relations with each BL6 booking in LA. I had begun working on publicity in the next cities on the calendar. TV producers, print and digital media journalists all required specific interview aid and coordination to maximize impact in metro areas around each city.

For influencers and bloggers, it was key to get them owned content exclusives no one else had access to. I loaded all coverage links and corresponding metrics into the in-house reporting platform so the group and managers had frequent updates and I could respond to each new question.

I also wrote and shared a list of English phrases and comments for each of the guys to practice for TV and radio show appearances. Again, everyone except Ki was pleased and friendly. In meetings and at the offices, he continued to be distant toward me. I decided that our lunch together was a one-time event.

But, a few days later, I was in the main corridor and Ki walked by, then turned toward me, "Oh, Mara. I have a couple of questions."

"Okay, what are they?"

He stepped a little closer to me and lowered his voice. "Actually, they're questions I don't think are appropriate to ask here. Could we take another lunch? Have you seen Seoul's trendiest neighborhoods?"

I said, "I'll be glad to answer any questions and I've taken one bus tour to see the city but haven't had time to explore."

At that point, I was happy that Ki was talking to me about anything. I noticed as he stood closer to me that I felt drawn to him like a magnet - his handsome face, beautiful eyes and lips, his tall slender body. I had to concentrate to sound professional. Again, my reaction surprised me.

"Mara, I'd like for you to experience some of my favorite neighborhoods while you're here. If you have time on Sunday and are interested, I'll take you to lunch at a café in the Hannam area and we can walk around. We could discuss your thoughts regarding my questions."

I was delighted, "Yes, I'm interested. I would love to do that."

"Good," he was smiling. "We'll be rehearsing on Saturday and part of Sunday. I'll text you with a time."

"Okay, I'll look forward to it."

♥

When I woke up Sunday morning, I was excited by the thought of spending time with Ki later. I wondered what we would talk about beyond business. I wanted to know more about him.

He texted me about 9 a.m. to say that he would pick me up at noon. Because it was a warm day, I chose to wear a fitted soft pink, sleeveless shirt and a short skirt in light gray, along with low-healed matching gray pumps. I had worn my hair in a French twist during the business week, but for today I let it hang loosely around my shoulders. It had natural curls.

Promptly at noon, Ki knocked on my door. He looked especially attractive in his light blue shirt and tan slacks. When I opened the door, he smiled and said, "You look great!"

"Thank you, so do you." A driver/bodyguard drove us to the Hannam shopping and dining area and stayed with the car while we went into a lovely restaurant nearby. Ki said it was one of his favorites.

Behind the building was a stunning area of lawns, flowers, towering trees and a pond with fountains. The view through floor to ceiling windows was soothing. There were tables and chairs among the gingko trees. We sat outside.

The menu was full of healthy options. Ki explained some of his preferred dishes. I chose one he suggested. He chose two additions so that I could try several recipes.

After we ordered, he asked me the business question he had in mind, "Would you be able to continue working with us during the rest of the tour, beyond the US leg? This is a thought I had, not something that management has mentioned. You're doing a great job for us so far and I would like to see it continue."

I knew they had concerts scheduled in the UK and Europe during this tour. Considering that their Korean PR manager was no longer able to do the work, the company would have to either keep me on or hire someone new after the US concerts were completed.

I said, "Thank you for the compliment. I would love to continue working with BL6 through the rest of the tour, and I believe I can be just as effective as I've been so far."

They were booked to perform in Paris, London, Berlin and Osaka before returning to Seoul for the final concerts. I continued, "I say that because, as you know, most business people speak English in each of the cities except Paris, which might be a little more difficult but I speak enough French to get by."

He said, "I know the rest of the band will feel good about you staying with us because they each have told me that they like working with you."

"That's nice to know."

He then added, "They all like you." His expression and tone suggested his simple statement meant more than it said.

I took a bite and managed only a "Hmmm," and a nod.

He then went on to say, "I know you must have a lot of pressure in your interactions with TV producers and journalists. How do you stay so calm and cheerful all the time? I admire that about you."

"Oh, thank you, Ki. I guess it's because my parents were very easy-going as I grew up. My dad was especially patient and kind. I saw them as role models. Our neighbors and friends were similar in temperament." I half-jokingly added, "Maybe it was because we lived in a small village surrounded by forests and farmlands. I think being in nature helps to calm people."

He responded with a broad smile, "That's interesting. I find that being in nature renews my psyche. That's why I like going to parks and beaches. Did you go into the forest regularly when you were young?"

"Practically every day. I loved the trees and wildflowers in summer and sledding in the snow during winter. It was a great place to grow up, although in the winter we had a lot of overcast days. I prefer sunny skies which is why now I enjoy living in California. How about you, did you have a forest or a beach nearby when you were a child?"

"I did. I visited both regularly. We have that in common."

We continued to talk as we finished our lunch, then walked around the neighborhood and looked in some interesting shops along the way. He told me how the neighborhoods of Seoul's Hannam region became popular over the years.

He also mentioned a funny encounter he'd had after hearing about it from friends, "There is a local man, Korean, maybe 70 years old, who dresses like Elvis Presley; and, blasting Elvis songs on his playlist, he often drives this gleaming 1956 gold Cadillac along the main street.

"In the evenings, he parks and talks with people who come by to look at the car, especially when they pour out of the bars at closing time with drinks in hand. He has many admirers in the community."

I laughed, "Sounds like a character straight from Venice Beach in LA! Ki, your mention of people spilling out of the bars reminds me of a question. I hope it's not too indelicate to ask. My cousin Bree worked here in Seoul. She noted how drinking was almost a professional obligation and that the bar scene can be rather intense as a result. Is that accurate?"

He said, "That is true to some extent but our company discourages drinking to excess or using drugs. During a dinner together, we might have a glass or two of wine or beer, just to relax. But that's usually the extent of it and we stay away from drugs."

"Good to know, thanks. Of course, LA can be intense, too. But I can't drink more than a couple of glasses of wine, then I'm in party mode. That's my limit. I've never liked beer or liquor much.

"That said, there is a craft cocktail called The Rose Hinted Glass at a spot my friends and I used to go to after work occasionally - I think it has Cognac in it. *One* of those and I'm... comfortably relaxed?" I think I blushed remembering a couple of those happy hours.

"The women I worked with there are so much fun! But, as far as drugs are concerned... I've tried marijuana twice. Even in this business, that's the extent of my drug use."

"That's another thing we have in common, then," he said. "We both value limiting liquor and drugs. But I have to admit that I'd like to see you 'in party mode.'"

I glanced away, now blushing for sure, but smiling, "Yeah, that's probably never going to happen."

He laughed, "It's fun to see you embarrassed."

We went on to discuss bands breaking up over drinking and drugs, then, to American music across years and genres. He was well informed. We each shared both humorous and serious stories, some from personal experience with colleagues in the business. We were relaxing more with each other and, at this point, easily talked and laughed together as though we had been friends for a while.

As we began the ride back, he reasserted the idea that I continue working with BL6 after the US tour. He said, "I'll discuss this with Hyun-Tae now that I know you're willing to do it."

I was delighted and thanked him again.

When we arrived at the building, after Ki walked me to my door, he said, "I appreciate your coming with me today. I enjoyed our conversation."

I told him it was a pleasure and went inside to prepare some business for the week.

Once at my desk, however, I had trouble concentrating because I was thinking about him – how handsome he is, his comments and generosity, how interesting he is, and on and on and on. I couldn't turn it off!

Still, I had no idea whether he invited me for lunch primarily because he wanted my work with his team to continue or is he personally interested in me? I decided it was best to consider it just another business meeting, with a thoughtful lunch added out of kindness. It had been a long time since a man had created this much emotional turmoil for me. I told myself, "Tune it out, Mara. Stay focused!"

♥

Something that I didn't find out until much later is that when we were walking and throughout our lunch, someone snapped several photos of us. They sold those photos to a news media outlet called The Blur that deals in celebrity gossip.

The outlet contacted BestStars and said either BestStars could pay them to kill the story or they would publish the photos with the headline, "Is BL6's Lee Ki-Yoon dating a Blonde American? Looks like it!"

BestStars paid them a large sum to kill it. In publishing, this is called "Catch and Kill." The executives, Choi Hyun-Tae and the security manager called Ki in to discuss the subject with him.

Ki told Hyun-Tae, "I'm sorry, so sorry that our lunch led to this problem. I remember last year when it was rumored that another idol might be engaged and he was attacked through social media by a lot of his fans. That would be a difficult and sad experience to go through. On the other hand, I'm 25, how and when will I be able to develop a serious relationship with a woman I'm attracted to if I can't even take her to a restaurant?

"That said, I asked Mara to lunch to see if she would want to continue working with us after the US tour. The band members think she's doing a great job. We all like her. I wanted to speak to Hyun-Tae this morning to see if he would agree to keeping her on. And, I admit, I find her interesting. I want to know more about her. I appreciate that you're talking to me and not her.

"I invited her for a 'business' lunch. It could be that she sees me, in a way, as her supervisor since I'm the BL6 leader. So, she might feel that saying no to an invitation would be rude. I hope you won't want to discuss this with her. She would probably feel that it's a reprimand when, really, it's my responsibility."

Hyun-Tae said, "She knows that her contract says consultants cannot date idols."

Ki answered, "I'm sure she didn't think of this as a date. She simply responded to my request. I told her that I had a business question that I wanted to ask, away from the office."

Hyun-Tae looked at the other manager, then said, "We won't talk with her. Just keep in mind that we may not be able to kill the next story if this happens again. I'm not going to tell you never to ask her out. But know that you're endangering your career and the band's key fanbase if they think you're dating, especially dating a blonde American. You're risking her career also, plus a lot of emotional pain for both of you."

Ki winced, "I wouldn't want that to happen. Thank you for reminding me of the gravity of the situation."

Hyun-Tae said, "Okay – that's it for now."

Ki left the office, saddened that he had caused such a problem for the company and disappointed that pursuing his curiosity about me had become so complex. He knew it was best to forget about having a personal relationship with me at this point.

K-pop Secret Love

2 *US Tour*

The next few days flew by. We were all working nonstop preparing for the concerts and, in my case, the PR preceding each of them. The BL6 members had become proficient in their radio and TV comments in English for LA and Chicago, the second stop on the tour.

American radio was a notoriously tough media for non-English speaking bands to break into. But I'd gotten them a key national spot that could open doors and establish the right tone for this tour. For BL6 to appear on some of the TV shows in LA, we were leaving on June 16th with their first concert scheduled on the 22nd.

While their social feeds were lighting up, I would be running local TV and radio ads that featured teasers for July's upcoming KCON LA – the annual K-pop convention where BL6 had pulled record attendance headlining the previous year. This way stans (K-pop speak for megafans) could build pre-sale excitement and be sure their friends and followers knew BL6 were stepping up to major venues this tour.

Everyone was focused. I hadn't heard anything more from Ki beyond what all of us discussed in the business briefings. We both behaved professionally toward each other within the company. I don't think any of the band members knew that we'd had lunch together a couple of times.

Three days before we were headed to LA, Manager Choi Hyun-Tae phoned me to ask if I would continue working with the company after the US tour. I told him I would be glad to. He said that he would arrange it with my PR firm in LA and add a new clause to my contract. I knew that my LA manager would negotiate an additional salary increase for me since I would be touring outside the US. I was excited.

At the start of my next meeting with BL6, Manager Choi joined us and told the band that I would continue as their publicist for the full world tour. All of them, Ki included, erupted in applause and "Bravos!" The enthusiastic reaction was great. I felt so appreciative that, subconsciously, I placed my hand over my heart, offering a deep bow. "Thank you very much." It felt like my *real* welcome to the team, amazing!

In the final days before The States, I was getting a jump on publicity for the Dallas and New York concerts. Arriving on an overnight flight from Seoul, the launch schedule gave us five days in LA for rehearsal and media appearances – including a well-publicized segment we'd be shooting on the streets of Korea Town – then the concert on the 22nd.

All of us were excited arriving at LAX. I had pitched that influencers, bloggers and print journalists encourage fans to be waiting at the airport for the BL6 arrival and had asked journalists to bring photographers.

There was an equal push across their social feeds. I told our security manager that I didn't know how many people would come out. The band members were very surprised when they walked from the plane into the airport and a large group erupted into cheers and chants, "BL6, BL6!"

There must have been three hundred stans there, ecstatic to see them. The airport had provided security to bolster BestStars' bodyguards.

The guys waved to the crowd, smiling and bowing. Favorable articles and photos flooded digital news and magazine feeds that afternoon saying BL6 had arrived, concert dates were listed. Ticket sales ramped up fast.

An entourage of about fifty people travel with the band – managers, the choreographer, bodyguards, back-up dancers, wardrobe personnel, make-up-hair stylists, photographers, even a male physical therapist who keeps the members flexible and conditioned for the intense choreography.

Since I was staying in my condo that night, my bags stayed in the van while we checked everyone into their hotel and BL6 prepared for their first nationally syndicated radio show that afternoon. Only the core crew, the managers, me, and their bodyguards went along.

On the way to the radio station, we rehearsed the English responses to questions the show's producer had hinted at – mostly playful stuff about visiting LA, favorite foods and cultural differences between here and Seoul.

I listened to the show with staff in the green room. The boys did a great job. Each of them said a sentence or two in English. While Ki spoke the most, he would encourage them to answer when he knew they had mastered a good response.

They seemed relaxed, made jokes and had fun – super professional. After giving them my congratulations at the studio, I texted each of them a specific compliment and got gracious replies. Their first national show was a success!

That evening I got together with my LA manager at the PR firm and all my co-workers for dinner. We had a wonderful reunion and spent the evening catching up and sharing stories.

The next morning, it felt great to wake up in my own bed. The familiar feeling of sun-warmed feet from the partial shade on my bedroom window made me smile.

I headed to the kitchen in my pajamas and started some coffee and oatmeal. The scent of the oats cooking brought thoughts of my dad.

When I was a kid, he often made my breakfast before I went to school. This morning I was making his recipe. He was my hero growing up, supporting my dreams and listening when I was upset or excited.

But here came the tears as I poured my coffee and filled my bowl with his oatmeal recipe - a bit of almond milk, honey, cinnamon and walnuts with the mandatory hot buttered toast for dipping.

When I was 17, it seemed impossible that my six-foot-four, healthy-looking, jovial dad would die within three weeks of being diagnosed with a rapidly-growing brain tumor.

The tears salted my first bites of oatmeal as I thought back to one of the days while I was staying with him in the hospital. Although he hadn't been able to speak much, he said to me, "Mara, go to college and *graduate*."

In a couple months, I was to leave for UCLA, a long way from my New York home and he must have been concerned that his illness would keep me in the village with mom. I still believed at that point that surgery would save his life.

I remember assuring him, "I will, daddy, don't worry." He smiled a little. That was the last thing he said to me. He died a week later, after exploratory surgery showed the tumor was too invasive to remove.

After his death I was hollow inside, a walking mannequin. I couldn't eat or sleep much. I lost weight. A few weeks into it, my mom suggested I use protein drinks each day to build nutrition. I missed my dad so much, especially our walks through the woods, full of laughter and long conversations. I felt desperately sad as I thought about him this morning.

That autumn I did go to UCLA where I had a partial scholarship. It was tough getting through some of the weekends when many students left the dorms and went home. Loneliness haunted me. It helped to Skype with my mom and my brother, FaceTime with Bree. My older brother, Dan, had been good to me as I grew up. Eventually, as I made more friends at college, life improved.

Most of the time I don't let my emotions overwhelm me. But this morning, being back in my little condo eating oatmeal, the sadness consumed me. Maybe my admiration for my dad was the reason I hadn't found a man I felt had all the characteristics that I could admire. I always found the men I dated lacking in some way.

I guess no one has everything we want in another person, nor everything we want in ourselves. I would like to be an ideal person all the time. But sometimes I don't have the knowledge, the strength or the will-power. Dad always had a way of getting me back on track.

By the time my oatmeal was gone, I could feel my blood sugar balancing out. I could hear dad saying, "Come on, Mar, you've gotten yourself that big client you wanted back when you first started college. Get out there and make a good day of it. Remember, I'm proud of you."

It's funny how you can hear someone's voice, clear as day, in your mind – even eight years after they've gone.

♥

I got on with the morning and looked forward to the hours ahead. I had an appointment later with a colleague at the firm who wanted to rent my condo and my car while I was away. He was neat and trustworthy, so I felt lucky.

That day, BL6 prepared for their first US Influencer segment with a veteran KCON vlog team. Even with all the Korean fame, this was their moment to make it pay off and claim their crowns as America's ult bias (a stan term for a favorite idol or group above all others).

It was a funny shoot because I'd inserted a standard clause in our confirmation agreements for each appearance to have some snacks and cold water in their "dressing room" per the band's request.

When we got to the outdoor shooting location, this super sweet vlog team of four women from LA and their two-man camera crew had stocked a huge cooler with water bottles and set up a folding table of snacks for the band. It was clear they'd paid for all this out-of-pocket and the guys were so moved. That made it feel like family. Everyone relaxed and had fun.

BL6 went beyond their adorably funny comments in English, which the vloggers loved, to give them something priceless. These girls are known for their K-pop covers and had over

400k followers on YT alone. So, Ki suggested that BL6 perform with them so the girls could do the choreography for one of their hits together. Not part of the plan but a total score – once San-A reposted on our feeds it had 850k views and 31k comments by sunset. Right on track, considering their VLIVEs were racking up an average of 1M viewers per stream by now.

After finishing the shoot and complimenting the band, I went shopping. I wanted to buy some new clothes for my European trip. I went to several outlet stores that carried name brands. Luckily, I was able to buy a hip, well-made suit with shoes to match plus a couple more skirts and blouses.

♥

The third day, BL6 prepared for their first TV show, a highly rated national network show. The host is a comedian. Both she and the guys made funny, memorable comments. She asked if they have girlfriends. Bin said, "We're too busy to date anyone."

The host said to Ki, "What about that beautiful blonde that I saw you talking with backstage." He laughed and looked embarrassed as he said, "She's our publicist, the company doesn't allow us to date employees."

The host followed with, "You looked as though you'd like to." The audience reacted with "*Wooo!*" Ki laughed, looked down and covered his eyes with his hand.

JJ then came to his rescue by saying, "We get plenty of love and energy from our fans." The stan-packed studio screamed their approval and applauded. The host then moved on. BL6 also performed a couple of their bigger hits. This first appearance on a national TV show spiked ticket sales for every date on the US tour. Yes!

By now, concert tickets were going fast, the arena in LA, which had 50 thousand seats, was almost full. Everyone was happy with my PR work.

More in-depth articles dropped the same day several blog features posted in both LA and Chicago. LA sold out afterward. The concert booker asked Manager Choi about BL6 adding a second show the next night. Through some miracle, the event booked on that date at the arena was postponed. BestStars and BL6 agreed, and over the next *two days*, the second show sold out as well.

After that, Manager Choi said he'd analyzed the earned media I brought relative to BestStars' investment of owned content and reported that our social shares and new followers were "epic." (For such a serious man, he could be dad-joke funny when you least expected it).

Then, he asked me if I thought the publicity I arrange could deliver a second show in *every* US city.

I said, "Based on the early numbers, if the social department and I heighten our coordination effort and are very strategic, then I believe it can." Game on!

He got us on a Zoom with San-A, the Social Media Director and then decided to try to arrange booking a second show in each arena – a matinee or evening concert. I appreciated his confidence in my work and the boost I was providing for the social team. At the same time, I was taking a risk by saying that my work could sell out a string of second concerts.

♥

I arrived at the opening concert with a backstage pass as well as a VIP seat out front.

While people were still filling the auditorium, I headed backstage to visit BL6's dressing room, wondering if any of the band members would benefit from last minute coaching on the short English phrases I'd drafted for each of them to use on this tour.

When I got close to the room, I could see that the door was open. After I took a few more steps, I stopped. I could hear Ki feeding the guys corrections and the pronunciations they needed before taking the stage. Even as Bin, Kwon, Sunny, Val and JJ were asking his help all at once, he was calm and patient in answering each of them.

Ki was taking care of them, in the best way possible, as the stylist worked on his hair. He was just as polite and considerate with them as he'd been with me during our lunches in Seoul.

K-pop Secret Love

Listening from the hallway, I realized that kindness is core to Ki's nature. It was clear that, after living and working with him for years, each BL6 member knew it. They knew they could trust him to be good to them, even pre-show, when most band leaders are super stressed.

My respect for Ki ballooned beyond what I had guessed about him during our two lunch conversations. His consideration for others wasn't temporary, it's who he is. I turned and walked back to my seat thinking about how both of us had the desire to help others succeed. This characteristic is my heart and we had it in common. I felt as though I knew Ki more deeply and it made me smile.

At the opening of the show, BL6 spoke the specific English phrases I'd rehearsed with them early on. They ended each of their comments with "I love you" or "Thank you for supporting us." The whole stadium was on their feet all night.

It was electric in a way I hadn't seen on any of my previous tours with other bands. These guys were magic. At the end of the concert, they all held hands, raised their arms high, then brought them down in perfect precision as they bowed. Confirmed, LA was crazy for them.

I loved each BL6 member even more after watching them perform live. Most of my clients had already met or passed their prime. Suddenly, I saw how far this group could go.

Because of the two-day booking, plane reservations to Chicago were postponed, giving all of us an extra day in LA. I got a text from Ki soon after we found out.

> If you'll let me and you have the time, I'd like to treat you to lunch at the beach in Santa Monica because you did such an excellent job at arranging our publicity in LA. It's been a great success because of your help.

> Thank you for giving me such a generous compliment, that means a lot to me, Ki. I would love to have lunch with you.

> You're well-deserving of the compliment. Would 11:30 tomorrow be okay?

> Yes. I'll be ready.

The next day, I wore white Bermuda shorts and strappy white sandals, along with a short-sleeved, yellow, V-neck knit shirt that was a perfect fit. The bright color seemed to emphasize the colors of my hair and eyes. Ki and his driver arrived at 11:30 on the dot.

When I opened my door, he had a big smile as he said, "Wow, you look fantastic!" I loved his irrepressible reaction. He was so happy that for a second, it seemed that he was going to hug me but he didn't.

I was surprised that his hair, which was blond during the concerts, was now black and he was sporting a very authentic beard and moustache. I said, "You look so different. I like it!"

He replied, "It's a disguise in case we run into paparazzi or fans."

"Well, it's a good one. I doubt that anyone would know that you're that blond guy who was on stage last night. You look great and very relaxed."

He smiled even more as we walked to the car and got in, "Yeah, I couldn't be happier with the way LA has gone. It was better than I imagined. I give your work the credit, so do the boys and the managers. They're thrilled with the added publicity we got. Your preparations did wonders for us."

"That's great to hear. Thanks for telling me." It meant a lot to me that Ki valued my work. Though Choi Hyun-Tae was my manager, Ki, as the leader of the group, had power in the company.

We cruised around Santa Monica, then into Venice. I showed him a few favorite spots and we stopped at the Rose Café and ordered a picnic – Venice-style – avocado toast with pickled chiles, their famous Rose Brunch Burrito and fresh-pressed carrot juices to keep Ki's energy high at the tour's start.

We drove to a quiet spot I knew in a little pocket of beach between Venice and the Santa Monica boardwalk. It has picnic tables shaded by a cluster of swaying palms.

Ki had bought a plastic picnic cover from the café for our table. With sturdy paper plates and utensils, we shared our lunch and talked, again non-stop. Ki offered our driver a plate of food which he took to a table several yards away.

Ki began by reflecting on the radio and TV interviews, how they went, his impressions. He was happy with each one and found them interesting from the standpoint of behind-the-scenes organization and communication.

He said, "During our first tour in The States, I was so focused on speaking English and playing full time translator for the boys that this is my first chance to truly observe the mechanics of American versus Asian media practices.

"You rehearsing the guys on English phrases and comments has made it easier on me, Mara, and made our interviews more interesting, too." I kept my immediate backstage flashback to Ki's pre-show coaching of the band to myself and thought, *his praise is generous!*

For the most part, he loved it. He said, "No matter how tired I get or whatever might go wrong, even though I worry about it, I really love being on stage. So much energy comes from the audience when we're up there. And, when I do my solo numbers, I feel great." Then he caught himself and, in a softer tone, said, "That probably sounds arrogant." He looked at me carefully for my reaction.

"No, you sound like a born performer. This is what you were meant to do and you're sending love to the fans when you're on stage, with your lyrics, your heart, the person you are. They love you! They want someone like you in their lives. You're an excellent role model for the kind of man girls should look for as a partner." I was speaking from my heart.

He looked at me with surprise and gratitude in his eyes, "That's kind of you to say. I deeply appreciate it and hope I *am* a good role model."

"You are. I have no doubt about it. I look at you and see an extraordinary man." (I could have gone on to say, "…that I could easily love," but, of course, I didn't. I stopped myself from saying anything more and was surprised that I was even thinking it. *Could I easily love him?*)

In the meantime, gentle breezes blew across the beach and us, making the mild warmth and atmosphere so soothing – I was home. The ocean had little white caps at the end of each wave rolling ashore. The scene, the weather, talking with Ki and looking into his beautiful brown eyes was mesmerizing.

Like me, Ki looked around, breathing deep, seeming momentarily hypnotized by it all. He murmured, "This is a beautiful place. I love it here."

Though I'd been to this beach many times, everything seemed fresh through his eyes and I realized I was delighted with every minute of being with him.

After talking about the LA shows, we reviewed what was coming up in Chicago. Then, Ki took the conversation in a personal direction again.

"You were telling me when we talked before that you and your dad got along really well, I'd like to hear more about you and your older brother...if you don't mind my asking another personal question." His eyes were soft, cautious.

"I'm happy to tell you about my relationship with my brother, but now that you've mentioned it, I'm curious about the reason you're asking these personal questions about my life" I said, smiling.

He looked a little surprised, "You're the only American I've ever had a chance to talk with about growing up in the US. Also, I find your personality and temperament intriguing. I've never met anyone like you."

"So, I'm an alien that you're investigating?" Now I was laughing.

"No, I'm sorry, I didn't mean to sound that way." As he spoke, he reached out and put his hand on mine.

In that instant, I felt the same connection and physical reaction I'd felt when we shook hands at our first meeting. We hadn't touched since then.

"It's OK, I'm kidding you." Then, I continued, "My brother and I get along well, we usually talk on the phone or Skype for an hour or so every week or two. And, his wife and I are good friends.

"Dan often has a different way of seeing a situation than I do. Sometimes, if I'm confused about something, I'll ask him a question about it and he'll give me an answer that I wouldn't have thought of but it fits the situation perfectly and clarifies things.

"I can't remember the last time we had an argument. It must've been in childhood. So, I love my brother very much."

Ki looked thoughtful, "That's beautiful, Mara. I'm afraid I haven't been that kind of brother to my younger sister. I've been so focused on my music and career that we haven't had many real conversations. I regret that."

I replied, "She probably understands. You'll have time in the future as you reach the heights that you want to scale, and I know you will. Then maybe you'll be able to slow down and have time to lead a more normal life."

He said, "I love the way you think and communicate, always so positive. Talking with you on this beach, with this breeze and the waves rolling in, feels amazing. I'm really enjoying it."

"Thank you, Ki, I'm enjoying being here with you, too. I'm so glad you invited me." Through all of this, he still had his hand on mine.

Soon, our driver motioned to us that it was time to leave. Ki lifted the containers holding the café's cinnabuns and French butter biscuits we hadn't eaten and said to the driver, "Would you like a dessert for later?" The driver seemed happy and returned the containers to their café bag. Ki put our plates, napkins and table cover in a trash bin.

On the way back, we chatted about LA. He said, "I love the year-round warm weather here. If I could, I would live here."

"Perhaps someday you will. If you do move here at some point, find me and maybe we could be friends."

He laughed, "Yeah, I would definitely like that."

For the third time now, he walked me to my door. Because I was staying in my condo, I invited him in for at least a quick look around, since he was limited on time.

He smiled as he looked at the rooms and said, "It's artistic, charming and very comfortable. It expresses your personality, Mara."

I said, "Thank you, I like to browse art fairs and find unique pieces by beginning artists."

I really wanted to hug him after our enchanting time together at the beach and his positive reaction to my home, but I was afraid that would be too forward, especially considering that the Korean culture places a high value on being respectful.

He did reach out, loosely intertwined his fingers with mine and said, "I loved our conversation today. It meant a lot to me."

"I'm glad." Just having his fingers touch mine caused an emotional reaction. But I hid the feeling. I had to keep in mind that Ki was like a manager to me. With that, we said goodbye.

Afterward, I phoned my cousin Bree and told her about our lunch and how I reacted again to his touching my hand. She is my confidant and it was time for a little perspective.

She said, "I believe there's definitely an emotional connection between the two of you. I think he feels it or he wouldn't be wanting to learn so much about you. Just be careful. You have to protect your career. Are you falling for him, Mara?"

I hesitated before answering, "I'm definitely attracted to him. But I know I shouldn't be."

Bree affirmed, "I think it's very wise that you're not taking any initiative. Continue to be very professional."

"I agree. I will."

That evening, I again met with some of my LA friends that I wouldn't be seeing for months now. They had a little farewell party for me in Malibu. The conversations and laughter were constant. One of the women teasingly said, for all to hear, "The guys in the band are so gorgeous! Which one have you fallen in love with, Mara?"

I laughed, "To be honest, I've fallen in love with all of them. They're not only handsome, they're also kind, intelligent and funny. The whole company has treated me very well and I love working with them."

Judy raised her glass and toasted, "To Mara, always the diplomat!"

K-pop Secret Love

3 Chicago, Dallas and New York

The first day in Chicago, BL6 met with me to review the influencer, journalist and TV booking schedule. Again, I coached them through clips of each host, reviewed how they interact in their interviews and memes their US followers or audiences love. We went through probable interview questions and each of them practiced answers in English.

Of course, I didn't have to practice English with Ki and we worked as a tag team coaching the others. We also reviewed key excerpts from the local press. They felt more assured after everything went so well in LA.

The next day at 6 a.m., they guested on Chicago television's most popular morning news show, performing a song with local, student dancers - the K-pop Dreamers - dancing backup. That afternoon they shifted to a special Chicago VLIVE from the road. Then, continued promo, doing back-to-back sets with the Windy City's superstar influencers. Each of the boys had mastered fresh, clever quips in English.

The rest of the time in Chicago went as smoothly as LA. They were amazing on all the local shows! A key magazine feature and the newspaper hype were very supportive. Tickets for their concert sold like crazy. And again, a second show, a matinee the next day, was added and sold out as well.

In Chicago, BestStars had arranged a fansign before the first show, where fans who have tickets to the concert can pay extra to attend an event with the boys in a stadium room a few hours before the show. Each of the 40-50 fans have about three or four minutes of individual time to talk with each member of the band and to have the guys sign their booklet.

Manager Choi and I were there along with the security manager and Gee Hak-kun, a talented member of the BL6 camera crew. Staff members attended to help move the fans, mostly teenaged girls, along the long table where BL6 sat.

Each fan went through a security check before reaching the fansign room. Some of the girls in line were ecstatic, excitedly talking with each other. Some were jumping up and down as they waited, still others were fixing their make-up and hair.

It was as though they were getting ready for a date. A few girls in the line, who were close enough to the open door to see the BL6 members started crying. I was surprised to see how intense their feelings were. I realized that some of them were obsessed with these handsome South Koreans to an extent that bordered on dangerous.

In K-pop, there seemed to be a notable intensity of aggression from some fans called sasaengs or sasaeng fans, meaning "private life" fans. I'd been aware of lone stalkers in the US. But I'd read that some of South Korea's more obsessive sasaengs have gone social, connecting with each other to organize serious threats or invasions of idols' privacy.

Most of the girls at this Chicago fansign were Asian-American and South Asian, according to BL6's security manager. He noted the tone as "super-charged" but said it didn't have "that dangerous edge, like some other events."

I asked him if they've ever had problems during one of these events.

"Yes, absolutely. One fan grabbed Bin in a bear hug and wouldn't let go. It took two security guards to pry her arms away from him while she screamed, 'But I love you!' Another fan tried to rip JJ's scarf from a tight loop at his neck, pulling him from his chair. She wanted to have something he wore near his heart.

"Although the boys get death threats regularly, most are not dangerous. But once we did take them off-stage and leave the arena because the threat seemed credible." His eyes never left the crowd as we spoke and, as we both surveyed the line, he added, "An idol in another group had a sasaeng in Seoul stalk him for many weeks. Finally, she managed to break into his house.

"Another was poisoned by a sasaeng backstage at a show. I did not manage that security team. Both females were arrested. These behaviors are now legal violations in South Korea and can carry prison sentences."

I said, "Those are extreme behaviors. I'm glad they're not common. Thank you for your work and for informing me."

Former clients of mine were no strangers to US stalkers and, to some extent, I'd known of fans being aggressive, even delusional. Hearing these details intensified my concerns about sasaengs. Really, the idea gave me chills. But in this business, you push such thoughts to the back of your mind, into a little room, and shut the door. The show must go on.

The whole time I'd been speaking with the security manager, Hak-kun was shooting photos and video, non-stop. The DSLR cameras used by BL6's crew seemed so complex. But when I mentioned this to Hak-kun, he insisted that even a novice like me could learn the basics quickly.

The BL6 members gave each fan they spoke with very comforting attention, laughing with them, holding their hands, giving positive advice if asked. Each of them was so kind, especially to the fans who were crying about something sad in their lives. Hak-kun got beautiful video, often with audible conversations that seemed priceless. He made sure fans' faces were not shown.

I'd started to notice that if I was particularly impressed with a photo of the group on stage or a portrait of one BL6 member, Hak-kun had taken that shot. He has an eye for balance, finding the spark or something candid without sacrificing ideal composition.

When the fansign was complete and we had a break while the guys prepped for sound check in the venue, I was treated to my first camera lesson. Hak-kun gave me a sort of 'DSLR for Dummies' session and had me take a few shots in the arena. He was right. It was easier than I'd imagined but I'd always been interested in photography.

♥

By now, double bookings for each stop had been added throughout the tour as a result of Manager Choi and other executives negotiating with arena managers and bookers. They were depending not only on BL6's popularity but also on my publicity to boost the social efforts and sell those tickets. I let all my New York contacts know how successful they'd been on the tour and we squeezed in added TV slots in NYC.

Continuing the airport precedent, I worked with BestStars' social team to be sure they'd have the fans and I'd have actual journalists (not just paparazzi) covering their arrival to growing crowds in every city.

That boosted publicity, even qualifying as local evening news in Chicago and Dallas. I'd begun lining-up publicity in Paris, the UK and Berlin – not entirely new to me as I'd supported world tours for my firm's long-time clients from LA's home office for a couple of years.

We had excellent success in Dallas. The shows were packed and smooth as glass.

Finally, we arrived in the Big Apple, New York City. As in the other cities, the publicity was great - the guys did key drive-time radio spots, major US YouTube Channels with social tie-ins and three major TV shows I had arranged. They thrived during each appearance. Back-to-back nights sold out. After the concerts, because of changes in flight schedules, we snagged a day off before flying to Paris.

Other than our group meetings, I hadn't heard from Ki since our last conversation on the beach in Santa Monica. Because I knew New York so well, I hoped to have the time to show him some of my favorite places. I was hesitant to contact him though.

Luckily, he texted me the day of the second concert.

> I'm getting used to this easy flow you've created for us. You're spoiling us, you know. We won't be able to work with anyone else... ever.

> LOL. Thx. I'm sure there are people as good or better than me.

> Mara, there's no one better than you.

I let that sink in.

> Thank you, Ki, that's a gratifying accolade.

> I know I'm asking at the last minute. Tomorrow I'm free and wondered if you would have time to meet for lunch and explore the city for a couple of hours.

> That would be great!

Ki had already seen the major museums in New York when he was visiting last year. So the next day, we had lunch at a beautiful restaurant near Central Park, which he had never seen.

We sat on the patio under swaying willow boughs where he ate classic American BBQ with fries and I chose a Cobb salad. A bodyguard came with us, staying a few feet away. Again, Ki wore his disguise – the cool beard and moustache – plus the standard bucket hat and dark glasses.

Most importantly in our conversation, Ki told me, "You're already influencing me. I called my parents and sister and told them how well the tour was going. I made a point of asking my sister how she is and said that she could call me any time that she wants to talk or ask me a question. I let all three of them know I'm aware I've been focused on my career and don't talk with them as often as I would like, but that I hope I can improve in the future."

"That's wonderful, Ki. I'm sure that meant a lot to them."

"It happened because of our conversations," he replied.

"I'm so pleased that our time together has been helpful."

He looked surprised, "It's definitely been very helpful. Just watching how you handle your work, staying stress-free and pleasant has been helpful. Does anything stress you?"

"Oh, sure, some things."

Ki said, "Like what?"

I smiled and looked at him, "You."

That made him laugh, "Me? In what way?"

"I can't figure you out as I have my other clients. I don't know the motive behind your desire to spend time with me. But I'm enjoying it … very much."

Ki had an amused smile, "I'm glad because I enjoy it very much as well."

I didn't say anything more because, based on his bemused expression, I felt that Ki could hear me thinking that my stress came from being attracted to him and wondering if he was genuinely interested in me. Is this relationship personal for him or just a curiosity and convenience?

♥

We walked in silence for a bit after leaving the patio, headed for my favorite spots in Central Park. We visited the bronze Alice in Wonderland sculpture with climbing children wearing the mushrooms smooth to gaze into the faces of the fable's characters. Their laughter added to the storybook environment.

Then we strolled to Bethesda Terrace. In the center was my favorite - a large two-tiered fountain with the transcendent Angel of the Waters at the top, striding forward, wings outstretched. She's surrounded by four cherubs at her feet representing health, purity, peace, and temperance. Ki loved the gorgeous eight-foot statue. A reverie we shared, viewing the plaza from every angle.

From there, we crossed west to John Lennon's memorial, Strawberry Fields, where we had a few minutes of reflection and Ki said, softly, "What an amazing artist … such a tragic end to his life."

Strolling north, above Sheep Meadow, we came to The Lake – it was dotted with lovers in row boats and surrounded by visitors of all ages from across the world. It's such a serene place.

There were toddlers running around with parents keeping a watchful eye, nine and 10-year-olds with little sailboats they were guiding on the water by remote control, and elderly people on benches chatting with one another.

We perched on the stone wall of a raised flower garden, just the right height for sitting, and enjoyed watching all the people in this beautiful scene. Without looking at me, Ki said, "I want children someday – when I'm traveling less. Do you think you'll have children, Mara?"

"I do. I feel the same way. I want to wait until I'm in my 30s when I have enough money not to work as much as I do now."

He turned and looked at me. Maybe I was imagining it but his eyes seemed to convey a loving feeling. It was as though he was continuing to chalk up the list of desires we have in common and he was especially happy about this significant one.

We talked easily, as usual. He told me some news I hadn't heard yet, "Because we've done so well in The States, doubling the number of concerts and income, the company upgraded our hotel and our rooms in Paris. The band is going to have an upper floor of suites. Managers will have rooms and offices on the floor below."

"That's amazing!"

"You mentioned that you've been to Paris before, right?" he asked.

"Yes, two years ago a couple of my friends were going and asked me to come along. We went to London for a week, then

Paris the week after. They had to fly home for work but my cousin, Bree, was visiting in the south of France at the time.

So, for the third week, I went South on a bullet train and met her. We stayed overnight in Avignon. Then, took a train the next day to Switzerland where we went up into the Alps on what looked like a toy train to the village of Wengen. It was a wonderful adventure."

"That sounds like a great trip! Do you speak French more easily now?"

I replied, "Just enough to get by. I got everything lined up publicity-wise between Google Translate and by speaking enough French for them to find someone in each office who could speak and understand some English. Nine French magazines around the country have already posted BL6 articles with photos that the social team is using, and you have radio and TV interviews scheduled with an interpreter attending each one"

Ki answered, "That's outstanding!"

"Thank you. When I visited France the first time with my two friends, just for fun, I learned the sentence, "Je parle seulement onze mots de Français.' It made us laugh."

He thought for a couple of seconds, then cracked up, "So, at that time, you could speak only eleven words of French?"

I laughed while thinking, *how many languages has this man mastered?!*

"That's right, and the only reason I knew the word 'onze' was because it was our hotel room number. I took French lessons *after* returning from the trip. Of course, they would have helped in several situations while there. But I was too busy to take a class before I left. I really love Paris."

We finished our exploration of Central Park and went into the Metropolitan Museum of Art. It was fun to be in a place we'd both visited before. We talked about the kind of art we loved best. For me, it's the impressionists and certain abstract works. For Ki, it's much broader and harder to narrow down although he appreciated my favorites as well.

By the time we browsed the Met's permanent collections and the stunning Temple of Dendur, hours had passed. We were hungry again and chose a nearby café for a light supper.

While there, I told him, "Bree and I got to see Van Gogh's collection when it came to LA for a few weeks while the museum in Amsterdam was being remodeled. After we explored every gallery of paintings and emerged into the California sun, we felt as though we were walking on air. The experience was a complete creative reset."

"That's the way I feel with visual art. We talked before about how nature seems to elevate our entire being, this seems to be true for me with art as well."

When we got back to the hotel, Ki said, "I'd like to avoid going to my room a little longer. Can I talk you into a dessert or wine in the hotel café?"

I said, "Sure," and, over strawberries, Champagne and classic New York cheesecake, we talked and laughed our way through the final moments of our time together in NYC.

4 *An Invitation*

By the following evening, we were in Paris. We had several days before the concerts. As a result, the band had a couple days off to sightsee before the interviews started. On the top floor of the hotel were BL6 members – some of the guys shared suites that had two or three bedrooms. Ki had a one-bedroom suite to himself.

In the halls were round-the-clock bodyguards, making sure that neither fans nor tourists could exit the elevators there. On the floor below were essential staff, including me. Other staff members and back-up dancers were in a less-expensive hotel. Besides our private rooms, my floor also included an office where I worked alongside others. Manager Choi shared a separate office with the security manager.

The next day, Thursday, I was on the phone with journalists and photographers to tie up final details on stories I'd pitched to them earlier. BL6 went to a rehearsal space to work through altered choreography for the Paris arena.

About 4 p.m., I had a briefing with them to share the latest information about interviews on French radio and TV. In spite of the interpreter for each show, on the plane I had given them French phrases to rehearse. Now, we practiced and I answered the few questions they had.

When the others had left the room after our briefing, Ki surprised me by inviting me to dinner for the next evening, Friday, in his suite at our regal hotel. I was confused. In my mind, lunch or sightseeing was one thing but dinner was something else - more serious - it seemed. Various thoughts rushed through my mind.

I thought there might be a business issue he wanted to discuss, as we had done with our lunches. I said, "I would love to have dinner with you. Should I bring any file folders on a subject you want to discuss?"

He smiled as though he was amused by my question, "No, I'm just looking forward to a relaxed evening of conversation with you. I'll come and get you about 7:30 if that's OK," he added. "I have a great view of the city from my windows, I think you'll like it."

Though my heart quickened as I thought, 'this is a real date,' I managed a calm, "Okay, Thanks."

I had enjoyed our lunches together. I liked that our conversations had been such an easy mix of business and personal exchange. During those hours, I felt a connection with Ki. He seemed very interested in me.

But he was interested in most people, especially Americans, as he explained when we were in California. After all, he was the leader of the group and in that role, I guessed that he felt he should know more about how I think. Still, we'd had so much fun and such meaningful conversations, this invite made me wonder if the connection was mutual.

After Ki left, I was the only one in the office and had some work to do, but my focus was out of control. Within a few minutes, Val came in. He was always a welcome break, very sweet. From just inside my doorway, he said in a soft voice, "Ki told me he was going to ask you to dinner. I hope you accepted."

I could tell by his voice that this was important to him.
I responded honestly, matching his quiet tone, "I did. But I don't know what to think of it."

He smiled and continued, "He likes you and I want you to know that it's been a long time since he has asked anyone to dinner or on a date of any kind. He hasn't talked about it, but I can tell that he's happier since you've been with us. I can see it in his eyes, especially when he's talking with you or about you. It's meaningful."

Now my mind was reeling. Val was telling me what I'd been wondering from the start. But I remembered I was talking to a man who loves fashion, so I shifted gears, "What should I wear for a casual dinner with one of the most loved men in the world? I mainly have business suits with me."

He smiled, his eyes lit up, "Let's go shopping! I know a little boutique near-by. The owner is wonderful, she'll have something that's perfect for a casual dinner."

And off we went, along with a bodyguard. The shop owner was a total *mom*, a very elegant French mom. She brought me several knockout dresses. I tried each one and chose a beautiful light blue dress with very soft fabric.

It had a low-cut, square neckline with tiny flowers around the fitted bodice. I walked into the store to get Val's opinion. From the chair where he was sitting, he beamed his broad smile the instant he saw me, saying, "It's perfect. You look beautiful! I know he'll love it."

"Thank you, Val." With that touching compliment, so sincere, I felt convinced myself.

The shopkeeper told me she could arrange an appointment for Friday in a nearby hair salon where my hair, now beyond shoulder length, could be styled into soft loose curls instead of the ponytail or French twist I usually wore at work. I made a late afternoon appointment.

As Friday began, I could barely concentrate; the day flew by with all kinds of scenarios going through my mind. What stood out though, were two of Val's softly spoken words, "It's meaningful."

I was excited to think that Ki may want a serious relationship with me. In the back of my mind, I had imagined it likely that he was romantically involved with a Korean woman in Seoul. There were so many exquisite-looking female K-pop celebrities that interacted with BL6 at various functions for groups of idols.

After my hair appointment Friday at 4:30, I felt and looked my best. I returned to the hotel by six. Between then and 7:30, I got dressed, put on a little make-up and kept reminding myself to *calm down, breathe*. My work doesn't stress me but a date with anyone new does – clearly, Ki was far from just anyone. Promptly at 7:30, there was a knock on my door.

Paris

When I opened the door, Ki looked at me in total admiration, "You look gorgeous! That dress is stunning on you and, wow, I love your hair that way."

I was delighted by his reaction. Of course, he made it easy to return the compliment in a loose silk dress shirt shaped by the clean lines and impeccable tailoring of an elegant grey suit.

"Thank you, and you look extremely handsome," I replied. We walked toward the elevator.

He said, "The boys went out early for dinner and sightseeing so we won't be running into them in the hall. They wanted me to go with them but I told them I was meeting a friend for dinner. Luckily, they were in too much of a hurry to question me further. They couldn't decide what to see first. By the way, what's your favorite part of Paris?"

"That's a difficult question. I love so many aspects of the city. I like exploring the unique neighborhoods, the architecture, the layout of the city, the museums. I'll bet that for you, the Louvre is your favorite place."

"Yeah, I spent days there when I was here before. The space seems endless. I love how even the ceilings of some of the galleries are masterpieces." Ki said.

Within minutes, we were at his suite. I was awed by the living room. It was truly beautiful, a flawless combination of Louis XV meets minimal elegance. The view gazing south from the Hotel de Crillon swept across much of the city with the Seine shimmering below us and the Eiffel Tower in the distance.

I heard myself saying out loud, "This is really magical!"

The dining table was next to bay windows. The furniture was traditional French throughout. The colors of the room were shades of pale gray and light blue, very relaxing. Ki's playlist was soft, romantic.

He said, "I thought we would have a drink and order from the hotel menu. I've heard that the chef is very good. I have some wine here. Do you have a favorite?"

"I enjoy Sauvignon Blanc."

Ki poured glasses for us and gave me a menu. We sat down on the sofa. I chose a petite filet mignon to match his full center cut and he phoned in our orders.

I took a generous taste of the wine to calm my nerves. It was delicious but I knew there would be red with the meal and wanted to stay clear-minded - alcohol goes straight to my head. I decided to savor it, slowly. That first swallow worked like a charm. Within minutes, I felt more relaxed.

Ki said, "I like how quickly you made a menu choice. Some of the guys take so long to order when we're at a restaurant."

"I haven't had beef for a while. It seems right for a dinner in Paris. Speaking of the guys, I'm amazed by how close you all are. Even though I'm sure you have your differences, from what I've seen, you're all very loving toward each other."

He smiled, "Yeah, I love them. They're like brothers. We've each said that we're closer than we are with our original families."

"I'd enjoy hearing more about your family, Ki, and life growing up in South Korea. How was childhood for you?"

He began, "My early childhood was easy. I was a good student. My parents liked that. They wanted me to go to college. But as you know from our previous conversation, as a teen, my interests shifted to music and rap.

"This caused difficulty with my parents; they were very much against my getting involved in rap culture. They didn't understand it. They had expected me to go into business the way my dad did.

"My mother, especially, was disappointed in me. After I joined BestStars without telling them, it took a long time for BL6 to build a following." As he said this, it seemed his eyes teared up for a moment.

"Anyway, my mom and I were in a battle for a while, a long while. But now that BL6 is more successful, she and my dad seem happy. During that period, though, the words that were said and the actions my mom took put some distance between us." With that sentence, a tear fell and he had to wipe it away. "I'm sorry," he said. "Those emotions came rushing back."

I was so moved by his tears that I put my hand on his arm and said, "Thank you for sharing that with me. I see it still bothers you."

He said, "I didn't realize it did until I said it just now. You seem to bring out my deeper emotions, things I guess I'm hiding even from myself."

Just then, our order arrived. The waiter wheeled in an ornate cart and presented dinner on exquisite china settings for the table – our appetizers, filets, potatoes, and salads. He poured merlot that was a flawless accompaniment to our meal and left a dessert menu on the coffee table. Ki told him that there was no need to come back, that we would phone if we wanted anything else.

While the waiter did his work, we sat on the sofa, talking. After he left, we moved toward the table.

Just before we reached our chairs, Ki turned to me and said, "There's something I've been imagining asking you for a while and I don't think I can wait any longer."

"What is it?" I asked, puzzled and definitely curious.

He smiled a little, looked into my eyes, and said, "May I kiss you?"

I think I stopped breathing for a second. He caught me off guard.

Beneath his gaze, I quietly said, "Yes."

He stepped closer to me and those incredible lips that I had been admiring for months were now gently pressing against mine as he slid his arms around my back. Waves of feeling rushed through my body.

He must have felt the same because the first kiss led to a second that was even more electric. This time he held my body more tightly against his. My heart was pounding. My feelings were almost overwhelming. Feeling his lips and body against mine was intensely exciting.

When we stopped, I managed to whisper, "Wow." He murmured, "That was amazing." We both laughed a little. He then pulled my chair back from the table so I could be seated.

He sat down, looked at me for a moment and said, "Let's make a toast." He lifted his wine. "To many more kisses in the future." We touched glasses. I said, "I like that idea."

We talked easily during dinner - more about our families, the difference in the cultures of our countries, what we loved or didn't about various cities, especially Paris, Seoul, New York and the towns where we grew up.

I said, "I'm observing how there is more emphasis placed on being polite and humble in Korean society than in the US. I like how thoughtful and considerate everyone is at BestStars, and how caring you and the BL6 members are compared to most American men our age. Not that American men are rude. But many seem to be more externally focused, going after their goals in a different way, some women too."

Ki said, "I've noticed that about various Americans. In many cases, I admire it. I learned about it to some extent when I got into rap and learned more while being interviewed by reporters and TV hosts, including women, I agree. In Korea, kindness and humility are vital aspects of our culture. I'm glad you admire that. Otherwise, you might consider me boring."

I laughed, "No, you are not the least bit boring. Being with you is a genuine pleasure."

He beamed, "I'm glad to hear that."

When we finished dinner, moved back to the sofa, and were still talking about family, I decided to tell Ki something I hadn't revealed.

"I told you about how close I was to my dad as I grew up. He was very supportive and would listen to my questions, answer every one, would console me when I was upset and always gave compliments when I did well. My mom wasn't like that. She was a good mom but not as supportive as my dad. We weren't as close"

Ki was listening intently, "Yes, I was impressed with your close relationship with your dad."

"Well, there's something I didn't tell you because it's sad and we were just getting to know each other. Anyway, I want to tell you that my dad passed away suddenly when I was seventeen." This time it was my turn to try to hold back the tears.

"Oh, no, Mara, that's very sad." He took my hand into his and kissed it.

"Dad developed a rapidly-growing brain tumor. The doctors told us that the location of the tumor made it inoperable. Within three weeks from diagnosis, he died. He was only 58 at the time. Losing him was heartbreaking for us. He was so loved and respected that 300 people came to the funeral home in our small town."

At that point, more tears were appearing. Ki put his arm around me.

I remembered I had tissues in my purse and found them to wipe my eyes. "I didn't feel that I could continue talking about my family without telling you about my dad's death. I didn't want to cry. I'm sorry. I probably look terrible now." I smiled, embarrassed saying that last sentence.

As he brushed a remaining tear from my cheek, he said, "You look beautiful, more beautiful than ever. Thank you for telling me about your dad. I know that can't be easy for you to talk about." At that point, he kissed me again, very delicately. Even that gentle kiss was stirring.

I said, "Thank you for being supportive."

I took another moment, and a deep breath, then said, "Now, let's move to a happier subject. I don't think I told you that when I was in Paris with my two friends, there was an afternoon when we had gone in different directions with plans to meet at Notre Dame Cathedral by 6 p.m.

"We didn't know that this would be happening but the children's choir was singing when we got there. Hearing their wonderful, high octave voices among hundreds of people sitting and standing in the cathedral was very moving. I snapped a photo of the choir that was ideal and I have the beauty of it emblazoned in my mind. It was one of those beautiful moments in life."

"That sounds very special. As you describe it, I can imagine the scene. I admire the way you move with ease from a sad topic to a beautiful one – another example of how you keep your thinking and emotions balanced. I want to be better at that."

He continued, "I get stressed with the responsibilities I have and keeping the team in good shape emotionally and physically."

I wasn't surprised to hear this. In the preceding weeks, I often wondered who was taking care of him.

He said apologetically, "I'm a worrier."

"Considering all of your responsibilities and all that you're doing, five or six jobs at once, it seems reasonable. You're allowed to be human."

His eyes studied mine for a second and he looked relieved, "Thanks for understanding."

He continued, "There's something more I want to share. The first years after BL6 started, we were struggling to build a fandom. I got a lot of hate from strangers on Twitter, mainly Koreans. Some people who knew me as a rapper didn't like that I had signed with BestStars, known for their Idol groups.

"Others hated the way I looked. Tweets telling me how awful I look came in regularly over the first years - truly mean comments, brutal names you can't unread. Some of the other guys had haters as well. It was constant bullying.

"I was young and had no experience at coping with this level of attack. I became depressed, anxious, and isolated with my thoughts. I didn't feel as though I could tell anyone how badly I was feeling about myself. I was bottoming out emotionally. As I got into gansta rap, I was angry and sad. For a while I didn't care if I lived or died.

"At one point, toward the end of a concert, I had a panic attack. I couldn't breathe and I couldn't go back on stage. After that, I wrote some very dark songs, trying to deal with thoughts of suicide. We Koreans rarely talk about therapy but I knew I had to do something or I wouldn't make it.

"So, I found a good therapist and went for weekly sessions for a while. It definitely helped. I then was able to share my experience with the band members and encouraged them to do the same. Also, I read self-help books to further support my emotions and expand my thinking." He studied me carefully now, "I hope that telling you all of this hasn't caused you to think less of me."

"Oh, Ki, not at all. I'm glad you shared this with me. It breaks my heart that you had to tolerate people being so mean to you. I admire your strength for enduring it and choosing to get help from a professional. I've known other celebrities who got therapy to deal with the brutal parts of fame.

"I hope you know by now that you are very handsome. I've seen photos of you online from those early days and you were handsome then as well. You have a stunning face and body." I took his face in my hands and ran my fingers across his brows, then kissed him.

He kissed me back, "I appreciate hearing that. I'm glad you think so."

I already knew from some of his lyrics that he grappled with life's bigger questions. But I didn't know that he had gone through such extreme difficulty in those early years with BL6.

♥

We decided to talk about lighter topics like pop music and American movies. Ki was delighted that I was a movie buff. He wanted to know my favorites. He hadn't had time to watch many American films.

We decided that on some evening we would watch an old classic, maybe Butch Cassidy and the Sundance Kid with Robert Redford and Paul Newman. But for tomorrow we planned to do some sightseeing during the day.

The evening went by in a heartbeat and after more conversation, Ki escorted me to my hotel room, held me in his arms and passionately kissed me goodnight at the door.

He said, "I loved being with you tonight."

I whispered, "I loved it, too."

♥

I began getting ready for bed while reminiscing about our discussions and those super-charged kisses. I had so many thoughts colliding after this one evening that I couldn't even tell you if I brushed my teeth. When I got into bed, I noticed a song had been playing in my mind.

As I was relaxing under my covers, I realized that tonight the song was 'Beautiful Disaster' by Kelly Clarkson. I had to sit up and immediately find it on YouTube. Sometimes I can hear a melody dancing in my head but don't even know what song it is. Then, when I recognize what it is, it turns out to be something that seems to come from my subconscious, telling me how I feel about what has recently happened.

Now, I read the lyrics.

One line describes the man she loves as someone who is spectacular but gets overwhelmed by his dreams. If she tries to have a serious relationship with him, it could be a disaster for her. Immediately, it was clear how this applied to me imagining a serious relationship with Ki.

I'm not supposed to get involved with the celebrities I work with. It's unprofessional and violates my BestStars contract, which is scary.

The song also asks "what is he after?"

Does Ki really care about *me*? If he were just another guy I'm dating, I wouldn't be so concerned. But he's a client; and I realize, as of tonight, that this relationship is becoming serious for me. I love being with him and when I'm not with him, I'm thinking about him.

I wondered, too, if I was bright enough to keep up with his intellect – the art, his insatiable reading of the world's great books. There's always something on his Kindle, stacks in his office. But maybe that isn't what he needs the most from me. He seems to need my calm demeanor and acceptance more, my emotional support.

Some women expect a man to take care of them financially and emotionally. I had grown up being very independent in both areas. I thought about how an independent woman would be good for Ki. He already had enough to worry about, he didn't need a clingy or a demanding partner to deal with and I didn't want that either.

My mind started meandering through my beliefs about relationships and life.

I believe in having a career, a relationship of equality, emotional and physical intimacy and in being emotionally supportive. I want a man to express his love for me in similar ways. And, I believe that people don't know each other very well until they've been together for three or four months, at least.

Plus, anyone can change as they go through life. These are some of the risks of entering a romantic relationship. It can be both exciting and a little frightening.

All these thoughts darted across my mind in seconds.

But, while still feeling the dreamy magic of being with Ki, I decided I'd think about my concerns tomorrow... or the next day.

I went to sleep smiling, with beautiful feelings that made my dreams glow.

6 *Monet's Gardens*

On Saturday, we decided to meet in the afternoon because both of us had work to do that morning. I started the day with a long shower and shaved my legs. I remembered having read at some point that most Korean men don't have much facial or body hair and *no* body odor. I know there were bullet-points explaining these random facts but I couldn't recall the science. The BL6 members had no facial hair that I could detect. Weird where your mind wanders while in the shower. Afterward, I got dressed and received a text from Ki.

> How's your schedule?

> I've wrapped up my work.

> Good, same here. We've both seen quite a bit of Paris before but not Monet's Gardens, right? Would you like to go?

> I would love to!

> Be sure to bring a hat and sunglasses. There will be a lot of tourists. We'll both need cover in case there are stans with cameras.

>> Got it. I'll bring them.

In a few minutes, we were in the car with BestStars security driving us northwest along the Seine into the French countryside.

It felt good to be with Ki again after last night, sitting close to him, feeling the connection between us. Before we left the parking deck, he kissed me a couple of times, then held my hand. We talked a little about the morning's work, then we discussed Monet's paintings, as well as others, and how much we each loved specific works of the various impressionists. As we talked, he kissed me a few more times. It was almost as though he couldn't look at me without kissing me. I loved it! Soon, we were at Claude Monet's country home.

Being in the serene Walled Normandy garden, among the flowers and trees, I felt immense romantic feelings toward Ki. I often felt like kissing him but I didn't. I wanted to be poised, test my patience. Also, there was a burly bodyguard walking a few feet behind us.

Ki was used to having someone around all the time; it didn't bother him at all. He kissed and hugged me occasionally throughout the afternoon and the sensation every kiss created was as beautiful as the one before.

Between the perfumed breezes from the flowers and Ki's kisses, I wondered at some points if I was going to faint! I know that sounds like something out of a Victorian novel, but it's true. I've never felt such overwhelming feelings in response to any man before.

Hak-kun's quick DSLR lesson from Chicago saved me more than once. Each time I thought I'd lose it, I'd use his coaching to get my left-brain logic back in gear, "Live View 1st, then hit Movie Record."

Somehow, recalling each sequence he'd shown me would sober me up and I got some great, candid shots of Ki, a few silhouettes with the bridge's Wisteria, roses and waterlilies on the pond, even a close-up clip where he glanced over and caught me filming by accident. He looked so sweet and genuinely embarrassed.

But Ki had no problem knowing I'd be FastBridging these shots to San-A in social at lunch. He even helped me crop them so they didn't show his beard or disguise. Sometimes this business is weird even for the people in it. But he and I both saw the practical side of things. So, getting the requisite images sent was all part of the day.

Again, we had great, nonstop conversation with some laughter in the mix. Luckily, no one recognized Ki, even with me taking photos. If they did, they didn't say anything to us or point phones in our direction. His hat, sunglasses and fake beard most likely helped.

About 7 p.m., we went back to the hotel suite, ordered-in and continued talking. By the end of dinner, we were feeling so close to one another after an idyllic countryside tour and a day filled with intimate conversation that when we stood up from the table, Ki put his arms around me, gazed for a long moment into my eyes and said, "I want to make love to you."

I took in an involuntary breath and could feel a reaction throughout my body. I didn't know what to say. I knew what my body was telling me, but logically, I still didn't know what to think of his motives, although he seemed very honest and sincere. I avoided answering directly, went playful and said, "But this is only our second date."

He replied, with a grin, "I thought you might say that. But, really, this is our 20th date."

"What?" Now I was grinning. "How does that logic work?" I was glad for the humor. We sat down on the sofa.

He explained, "We've had four lunch dates, also four sightseeing dates, and about ten meetings that lasted an hour or more, as well as our hours-long dates yesterday and today. Those totals in hours create an equivalent of 20 dates."

"The meetings and the lunches were business." I noted in mild protest, as he kissed me again.

He continued in his serious tone, "But during every meeting and lunch, I developed a stronger and stronger interest in you, felt more attracted to you each time and couldn't stop thinking about you afterward. I've written four love songs about you in the last week. This kind of strong reaction toward a woman hasn't happened to me till now. For me, this is serious. I feel like I'm falling in love with you."

I blinked a few times listening to Ki's statements. It took a few seconds to let this information sink into my mind. He was looking at me so lovingly that all I could do was whisper, "Yes."

I went into the bathroom, took off my blouse, skirt, and shoes. I had on a sheer lace bra and matching low-cut lace panties in a nude shade. I took a few deep breaths and felt glad I still had my IUD.

When I came out, Ki was standing next to the bed in black bikini briefs and had turned down the covers all the way to the bottom. His eyes softened when he saw me. He was gazing at me with such care that I immediately embraced and kissed him. He's several inches taller than me. So, I was looking up at him and began feeling like a young girl who had never been in love before.

As he looked at me, he said, "Mara, you're so beautiful." His hands gently slid the straps of my bra off my shoulders, I was filled with intense desire. With his hands on my arms, he said with concern in his voice, "You're trembling. Are you afraid?"

I spoke softly, "No, it's anticipation."

He was tender as he picked me up and laid me on the bed. I unfastened the front clasp of my bra, exposing my breasts. From the side of the bed, he admired me for a moment, then removed his briefs, moved on top of me and began kissing me, all of me - my lips, neck, then my breasts, spiraling his tongue around my nipples. He moved down my body, kiss by kiss, generating sparks every inch along the way. He slowly removed my panties, kissing my hips and inner thighs. The feelings flooding through me were so intense that I barely noticed the soft sounds of pleasure that I was making.

I felt my mind and body surrendering to him, completely.

He cupped one breast in his hand, kissed and licked it, then the other. I ran my hands down his back, over his smooth skin. His hard penis pressed against me between my legs. I felt as though he could do anything and I would love it.

Effortlessly, he slipped on a condom. He gently pushed inside me and began to slowly move back and forth. We belonged to each other, we melted into each other.

My breath quickened and I opened my legs wider, he went deeper, moving with more intensity, exquisitely. We were breathing hard and gasping with each thrust. Within minutes, my orgasm began. I was floating, thoughts dissolved, sensation consumed me. We climaxed together.

A waterfall of pleasure drenched my senses. My nerve endings were tingling and I felt so good that I didn't want it to ever end. I kept my arms around his back, his face was to the side of mine. We were both still breathing hard.

I then slid my hands from his back to his face and felt tears. Surprised, I whispered, "Are you crying? Are you disappointed?"

He pulled away then, onto his side, propped up on his elbow. He wiped the tears away and smiled, "Sorry. My emotions are overwhelming right now.

"I'm happier than I've ever been! And not only because of the amazing sex we just shared – it was extraordinary - but Mara, our time together, our conversations and laughter… I haven't been so excited and yet so relaxed in years. The person you are… I've been dreaming about you for a long time, hoping to find you. And now you're here."

His face became more serious then and he said softly, "I'm in love with you. I want to spend every minute I can with you. I've never felt so good with anyone." His eyes were looking intently into mine, looking for a sign of my response. "I hope you feel the same."

After being mesmerized by his inspired declarations, I said, "I've been falling more in love with you every hour that we've spent together and the way you made love to me just now created the most incredible feelings I've ever felt."

His pensive expression turned into relief and exhilaration, "Mara, I'm so glad!" He gave me a long, magical kiss. It seemed that I could feel his happiness radiating from his lips and body into mine. He didn't seem to have a single doubt about our future together. But I did.

After this kiss, I said, "It's tremendous - the way you're looking at me right now. I'm glad that I can bring you such happiness. I'm glad that you love me. At the same time, I have to admit, I have some concerns."

He immediately sat up into a crossed-legged position, facing me, pulling part of the sheet across his lap. Magic gave way to reason and I watched the problem-solver in him take charge. "What are they?" he softly asked.

I propped pillows behind my back against the headboard. Calmly, I said, "I'm concerned about what management will say. As you know, there's a rule against employees, even consultants, dating BL6 members.

"Secondly, what if, after a few months, you change your mind about me?

"In either case, I could be fired, which would damage my career in general. Because I've worked six years in this business, including my internship, and have a good professional reputation, I don't want to harm that. I hope you understand. I love you, Ki, and I do want, very much, for us to build a relationship that endures. But I also want to protect my career."

He took my concerns seriously and said, "I feel as though I need to talk with Hyun-Tae about this tomorrow. I want to protect your career as well and clear your fears about me changing my mind - I know that's not going to happen. But if for some strange reason it did," he smiled, "like I discover you were a BitCoin hacker in your earlier life – we could ask the company to add a clause to your contract saying they will keep you employed, if you want that, or guarantee that you leave with the highest recommendation."

I was pleased with his ideas.

"Thank you for being so considerate, Ki." I felt heard and loved. It had been a long time since I had anyone helping me with my career. It felt good.

We then relaxed and lay down. Ki held me in his arms and said, "I want to love you and, when you let me, take care of you. Mara, I'd like for us to move in together, like, tonight?"

Inwardly, I felt my heart and soul say, *Yes, that feels right!*

But I took a second. "Ki, do you mean what you're saying? Because, it's a huge decision."

When he said, "Yes," - there it was - clarity, zero hesitation – I knew, right here in this Paris hotel room, I was home…in his arms.

With that declaration and a few minutes spent floating in this perfect dream, we were asleep.

Luckily, I woke up about an hour later. He was still sleeping. I knew I didn't want to be seen in the morning by the bodyguards in the hall or the guys coming out of their rooms, so I quietly got dressed and wrote Ki a note: "Tonight was amazing. Tonight was for us. I've gone for now so we can keep it that way. M."

I left, shutting the door as silently as possible. It was still a reasonable hour for ending a date. A couple of bodyguards were talking together at the entrance end of the hall. They didn't look my way. I went down the staircase to the lobby and took the elevator to my floor. I made it to my room, undetected.

Once inside, I continued thinking about the extraordinary day and evening, of feeling Ki's love for me and experiencing the beautiful love-making that took us to such a deep level of intimacy. I hoped that this was the turning point in my life that I had been longing for - a close, loving, enduring relationship that could work for both of us.

7 Introductions

The next morning, a sunny Sunday, my phone rang at 8 a.m. Ki said, "Good Morning, I hope I'm not calling too early. I loved our evening together and I deeply love you."

"I'm so happy that you love me. I love you, too, with all my heart. Being with you last night was magical. And, it's not too early."

He went on, "I woke up dreaming about our time together, wondering if it really happened. When you weren't here, it scared me for a second until I saw your note. Then I knew I hadn't dreamed it. I felt so happy.

"Today, I hope to take you to brunch and do some sightseeing. But first, I have a meeting with Hyun-Tae to discuss what we talked about last night. It's here in his hotel office. Then, I've asked the boys to meet with me in his office after he leaves. Beyond that, you and I can make plans for this afternoon – whatever you want to do."

"That sounds perfect," I answered and I meant it. I knew, that instant, that Ki's conviction to our love required no professional worry on my part.

In another K-pop management company, announcing this relationship might be like a bomb going off. But with Ki and the guys, it was clear they were in a good place for this and the team was solid. I knew he would manage it very well.

It felt great to realize I didn't have to be concerned. Things were going to go well.

So, Dear Reader - Happily, I wasn't part of the next conversations. But Ki filled me in later. From the details he shared, this is how I imagine they translate into English.

Ki met Manager Choi at his temporary office in the hotel. As they went inside, Hyun-Tae said, "Ok, Ki, what's so important that we have to meet on Sunday morning." He sat down in the chair behind his desk and Ki sat across from him.

Ki began, "Sorry to take your time today but I need your help. I have a request. And I need to start by saying that, in spite of the photo incident in Seoul, I've spent more time getting to know Mara."

Hyun-Tae shifted in his chair but offered no reaction.

"To avoid another photo, when we've gone out, I've been using a beard and moustache disguise, plus hat and glasses. We've had several more lunches together in the US as well as long periods of sightseeing.

"This week, we spent all of our time off together. We've had many hours of meaningful conversations. I realized during this past week that I'm in love with her. I want to have an ongoing, serious relationship with her.

"She's concerned about her contract with the company. I want to protect her and am humbly requesting that you make changes in her contract that will do that."

After taking a moment, Hyun-Tae finally responded, "Whoa. You're shocking me with this!

"I'm not happy that you've continued to date her; but, mostly, I'm surprised because I didn't think you'd be the first one in the group to get serious about a woman. I mean, you boys have had various, brief romances. But you've been the one with the least involvement. You've been such a driven workaholic during these years."

Ki replied, "Yeah, I knew you'd be surprised. But I've written four love songs in the last week. They're good. I didn't have to agonize over every word, they just flowed."

Hyun-Tae laughed. "Oh my God, you ARE gone!"

Ki grinned and glanced skyward. "I am. It's true. Honestly, I've *never* felt this way before."

"Okay, I'm going to sound like your dad right now because he isn't here," Hyun-Tae responded. "I'm going to ask you some hard questions because you're like a son to me and I don't want you to get hurt. Ki, millions of women would love to be in a relationship with you or any of the other boys. Did you - or Mara - initiate the relationship?"

Ki said, "I've initiated everything. She's been *very* professional during our time together. When I asked her to dinner for Friday, she even asked if I wanted her to bring any business folders. I had to *tell* her that it would be a social evening."

"I've taken the lead in every aspect of this relationship. Actually, I was intrigued with her from the moment she walked into the conference room in Seoul on her first day of work."

Hyun-Tae listened intently and said, "Please don't misunderstand me. I respect Mara, she's doing a great job for us. She's professional and smart. In fact, now that I think about the two of you together, I can see how your personalities could be a match. Has she said that her feelings for you are as intense as yours seem to be?"

"Yes. After I told her that I'm in love with her, which happened last night, she said she feels the same about me. Every time we've talked together, I've made a point of learning more about her background, her likes and dislikes, her beliefs and dreams for the future. We were very comfortable with each other from the first time we had lunch. We seem to be very compatible."

Hyun-Tae went on, "When are you going to have time to spend with her? You barely have time to spend with the boys unless it's a scheduled, company-filmed outing?"

"I know. I'll figure a way to work it out. You have a family. You're doing it." Ki said, looking concerned.

Hyun-Tae replied, "But I don't have the creative talent that drives you so hard. You spend most of your free time writing lyrics. Also, I don't have five 'brothers' who want my time and attention to the extent that they want yours. Even so, often my family feels neglected because of my work."

Ki was thoughtful now. "I only know that I've been hoping to have a woman like Mara in my life. I can't lose her. She's so easy to get along with. I've never seen her upset or stressed about anything. And, if you can work out the contract changes, she'll travel with us. We can stay together in each city. That gives us some time with each other, daily, and you'll save the cost of at least one hotel room." Now Ki flashed a knowing grin.

"Another thing," Hyun-Tae said. "Is this girl from sunny California going to be happy living in cold, dreary Seoul in the winter months? Right now, it's summer, but November through March, even Koreans get depressed."

"Yeah, I thought about that. We haven't talked about it. She grew up outside of New York City and didn't like the cloud-cover there in winter. I can afford to offer her travel to California several times during the worst months to get some sun and see her family and friends."

Hyun-Tae continued, "You know that we have to keep this a secret as we have with the other relationships you boys have had. Is she okay with that?"

Ki said, "Yes, that doesn't bother her. In fact, she said she doesn't want to interfere with my career or time with the guys. She realizes that this isn't going to be normal. She knows how we work. She's very independent. She works long hours herself, keeping a similar schedule for her clients."

"What about protection during sex? You're both smart, so I know you must be using something," Hyun-Tae said.

"It's taken care of, neither of us wants children until we're in our thirties," Ki responded, knowing how Hyun-Tae's management style covers every concern.

The two men looked at each other for a few moments.

Hyun-Tae then spoke with a grin, "I really didn't think you'd be the first. But, obviously, you're there – and with a blonde American! Whew, when the press discovers that you two are a couple, they'll tear you apart, Ki. It's going to be difficult for both of you. But, knowing you, it doesn't surprise me that you would fall for a foreign girl. You often make the unusual choice."

Hyun-Tae then smiled sincerely, "I'm glad for you, Ki. Although it'll be a struggle in some ways for each of you, I want you both to be happy. You deserve to be loved by a woman who has your best interest at heart. From what I know of Mara, she's very thoughtful and giving.

"Yeah, the more I think of the two of you, I think she will be good for you. I've noticed that you've been happier, I just didn't take the time to figure out the reason." Hyun-Tae paused a moment, then said, "I'll take care of the contract. Have Mara send me an email detailing the changes she wants."

Both men stood up and hugged each other. Ki said, "Thanks, Hyun-Tae. I appreciate this."

"Have you told the boys?"

Ki answered, "I plan to do that in a few minutes, here in your office."

"What about your parents. How do you think they'll respond?"

"Hey, as you know," Ki said, "My parents realize that they have a son who has never done what they wanted, but it worked out well in the end. Hopefully, they'll trust me on this and will be opened-minded."

With that, Hyun-Tae gave a nod and left the office. Ki waited for the boys to arrive, which they did during the next few minutes. They each took a seat around or on the desk.

Ki began by saying, "Thanks for meeting with me on your day off. This won't take long. I want to tell you something important for the sake of honesty."

Each of the guys was looking at him with concern and curiosity, waiting for his next words.

He began, "I want to explain this in a short summary and then you can ask questions if you have any. Starting in Seoul, I felt a connection with Mara and have been having lunches and sightseeing dates with her during the tour. We've had a lot of good conversations and I've gotten to know her very well.

"On Thursday, I asked her to dinner for Friday in my suite. We again talked non-stop. We also spent most of yesterday together.

"I told her last night that I want to have an ongoing relationship with her and talked with Hyun-Tae about it this morning so that she's protected from company rules through a clause in her contract.

"He agreed, and now I'm telling you so that you'll know what's going on. I've asked her to live with me as we continue the tour and when we get back to Seoul. She said 'yes.'"

At this point, Ki was smiling as he watched the faces of the 'brothers' he knew so well. There was a moment of silence.

Then, Kwon, who looked puzzled, spoke, "So you're in love with her; you've told her that; and she's in love with you?"

Ki smiled, "Yes, we shared our feelings for each other yesterday and I told her about my desire for us to live together."

The boys had been quiet during his quick speech, some were smiling, some seemed a bit stunned. As soon as Ki answered Kwon's question, they all began talking at once.

Val was smiling and said, "I'm glad! You'll be good together."

Bin exclaimed, "How did I not see this coming? I haven't even seen you having lunch together or being together at all. Oh my God, Ki, I'm shocked! It seems fast for such a big decision. Are you concerned?"

Ki was steady. "No, I feel certain about this. I was attracted to her the day she arrived and outside of our meetings, I've spent many hours with her in non-stop conversations.

"There hasn't been a moment that I've felt uncomfortable; and we've had some deeper sharing about our families, our past experiences, our beliefs and our hopes for the future. She's the kind of woman I've been dreaming about for a long time. I don't want to lose her. She's beautiful, smart, and easy to get along with. She's not like any woman I've known before."

Bin said pensively, "She does seem extraordinary."

JJ stood up and gave Ki a hug, "I'm happy for you, Ki. I've noticed that you've been more relaxed during the past weeks. I wondered if it was because of Mara. I saw you having dessert with her in our New York hotel café as I came in.

"Seeing how much you were enjoying each other held my attention. I watched the two of you for a few seconds. You were talking and laughing together like two people in love. I'm glad."

Ki hugged JJ, "Thanks, you were right. By the time we were in New York, I knew I was falling in love with her. We spent the day in Central Park. Since Seoul, every time we've been together, the relationship has become deeper and more meaningful."

Kwon smiled and hugged him, "That's great, man! I wish you the best."

Sunny hugged him too and congratulated him, then asked, "How are you going to do this, I mean, your schedule is so full all the time already?"

Ki said, "I'll work that out. I don't want to reduce my availability to you guys. She understands that my work with this team is very important in my life.

"At least, I have the advantage of her traveling with us. She wants to keep her career going with our company. Her schedule requires long hours also, which helps. The beautiful part is that when I come home at night, she'll be there, no matter where we are in the world."

Bin said, "Wow, that sounds great!"

Ki went on, "And, as with any relationship that any of us has had in the past, this has to be kept secret."

By now, Ki was eager to get back to me. He asked the guys if they had any other questions.

Bin said, "Sure, I would like to ask more, but I won't at this point."

Ki smiled, "Okay. Thanks for the support and the good wishes." They each hugged him as they left. He then texted me and said that the meetings went well and he'll be with me in a few minutes.

♥

While Ki was with his manager and the guys, I gathered my cosmetics and a few clothes from my hotel room and moved them to Ki's suite, which had plenty of space for a second person. There was even a second bathroom which easily stored all I'd brought.

When he returned, it was about 10 a.m. He walked in beaming, came over to the sofa, sat down and kissed me. He said, "This feels so good, coming to my suite and seeing you here. I love it."

I laughed, "I love it, too. We're going to have fun together. Love, conversations and fun instead of nothing but work."

"I agree," he said. "I can't even express how happy I am that we've reached this point."

Ki told me the details of the meetings. We were both pleased that everyone was supportive. It meant so much. Each of us had our own reasons. For Ki, BL6 is his family. For me, my job and career will be safe. Neither of us wanted our relationship to upset the closeness of this band of brothers.

Ki said, "There's one more thing I want to do before we go to lunch, tell my parents and sister what's happening. I would like to introduce you to them by Skype today if that's okay with you. I'll tell them that we've been dating for a while and that I want them to meet you. It will take only a few minutes."
I asked, "So, at this point, you don't want to tell them that we're living together on the tour?"

Ki seemed confident. "No, I don't think they need to know that right now. Just knowing I'm in a serious relationship is enough for them to hear. After I talk with them for a few minutes and explain the basics, then I'll introduce you."

"Do you think the fact that I'm not Korean will bother them?" I was trying to think through my immediate considerations.

"It might bother my mom a little, probably not my dad."

Suddenly, I thought about the casual clothes I was wearing, "Ki, I'm going to quickly change my clothes."

Ki said, "You look fine." I was already up and moving toward the bedroom closet.

"It'll just take a few minutes. I need to wear something appropriate for this occasion. It's important. I'll be right back."

I quickly changed into a white, tailored blouse and a navy-blue skirt, then returned to the living room and sat in a chair a couple of feet away from Ki. I put on a simple gold necklace under his patient gaze. "Okay, I feel a little nervous, but I'm ready. Let's do this!"

Ki sighed, "I love you. I realize that I'm rushing you into this first meeting, but it'll be helpful for the future if I let them know sooner rather than later. You look great."

First, he texted his parents to see if they were available. They answered right away that they were. At the start of their

Skype, they spoke in Korean. When he saw them pop up on the screen, Ki smiled and said, "How are you today?"

"We're healthy," his dad answered.

"Is Sis available to join us?" he said.

"Yes, she's here. Are you all right?" his mother asked as his sister came into view.

"Yes, I have something I want to tell you. Back in April, our company hired a new publicist for our US tour. She's an American. I thought she was very interesting. I began asking her to lunch and sightseeing. We've had many in-depth conversations as we traveled across the United States. She also speaks Korean.

"Just in the last couple of days, we've decided to become more serious about our relationship. For that reason, I would like to introduce her to you."

There was a moment of silence, then his dad said, "Yes, Son, of course, we want to meet her."

I walked to the sofa where Ki's family could see me and nodded, ceremoniously, toward them. Ki's father bowed as his mom and sister nodded in return.

I said in Korean, "It is an honor to meet Ki-Yoon's family." Then, I sat down next to Ki.

He said, "This is Mara Jansen."

I said, "You have a wonderful son."

His mother answered, "It's good to meet you. We have a son who sometimes surprises us."

Ki said, "I wanted to call you today and introduce Mara to you so that you know what's happening in my life. When we're back in Seoul, after the tour, we can have dinner together at the condo so that you can get to know her more fully."

His mother said, "Mara, where in America do you live?"

"I live in Los Angeles, California. But I grew up in a small town in the countryside a few miles from New York City."

She asked, "Does your family live near you?"

"My mom lives near my older brother, close to San Francisco, which is a couple of hours away from Los Angeles by plane. I visit them often. While I grew up back east, my parents owned a grocery store for many years and were well-loved by the people in our town. They were known to be kind and honorable.

"Unfortunately, my wonderful dad passed away from cancer eight years ago when I was 17. I still miss him. My older brother is a certified home builder. He's married and has two young children. We're a close family. We enjoy each other's company."

His mother said, "It is sad that you lost your dear father. Thank you for telling us about your wonderful family."

I told her, "I'm happy to answer any questions that you might have about me or my life. I understand that it is probably surprising to learn that your son has started a relationship with someone you don't know and who isn't Korean."

His father then said, "We want our son to be happy in his life. We wish you both much happiness together."

Ki said, "Thank you, dad. That means a lot."

At that point, Ki added, "Sis, do you have any questions you want to ask?"

She said, "When will you be back in Seoul?"

He answered, "In about a month. I'll keep in touch with you and if any of you have further questions for me before that time, feel free to call, text or email me. I'll be happy to answer."

With that, Ki said that it was good talking with them, we bowed, and he said we would see them soon.

After we ended the call, I looked at him, "I think that went well. Your parents seem nice and they look so young. Your sister is very pretty."

Ki said, "I'm glad you think it went well. I appreciated my dad's good wishes for us. My mother will probably have more questions. That's the first time I've ever introduced any woman to them. I'm sure they were surprised and know you must be very important to me."

He then put his arms around me, kissed me and said, "I'm certain you made an excellent first impression. They'll like you very much as they get to know you."

We decided to find a café for lunch, then roam the streets of Paris, as well as check to see how long the lines are at the Louvre. First, I quickly changed back into my casual clothes.

Ki wore a bucket hat, dark glasses and his beard and mustache disguise, hoping no one would recognize him. We took a bodyguard, the company required that of each of the band members during the tour.

Sandy N. Olson

8 *Deeper Discussions*

Emerging from the hotel in the 1st Arrondissement, the delight of its cream-gray Paris limestone under blue skies was immediately enchanting. With the Louvre to our east and the Grand Palais to our west, Ki asked if I'd like to stroll through the Jardins des Champs-Elysées and find lunch along the way.

Once we'd settled in an outdoor café halfway to the Bois de Boulogne, Ki asked, "When will you tell your brother and mom about us?"

"During the week. I'll Skype with them and explain how our relationship developed over the past weeks, that it's now become serious and that we've begun living together. Then, I'd like to let them know that they can meet you by Skype, whatever day works best."

"Absolutely! Do you think there'll be any problems?" he asked.

"The only problem I can think of is that they'll be concerned that I'm not coming back to California as soon as they thought I would. But for the most part, I'll be living in Seoul until we're ready to travel again on the next tour."

Ki was sitting close to me at our small round café table. He looked concerned after my statement, took my hand in his and kissed it, "I don't want to deprive you of seeing your family. Anytime you want to, you can fly to California to visit them and if I'm free, I'll be happy to go with you.

"I won't have any problem paying for anything you need or want. Remember, you earned press that doubled our bookings on this tour. As far as I'm concerned, the money I'm being paid for these months is *our* money, as is everything I have. We earned this tour income as a team.

"Mara, we haven't talked about how we'll manage money. I know that some couples split the cost of living. But in our situation, that is unnecessary. I would love to take care of you in every way possible. At the same time, I want to do what allows you to feel comfortable."

"Ki, that's so generous! The visits to California are very considerate. My family will be happy to know that I'll see them soon and I would love to have you come with me when you can. As far as money is concerned, I've been financially independent for years so this will be a bit of an adjustment."

I continued, "As you've said, we haven't talked about money. So, I'll share some details about my financial situation. It's important to me for you to understand that part of my life. I've always lived within a budget.

So, let's see... My credit score is excellent and I work to maintain it. I own my small condo in LA owing to last year's low interest rates and the money mom gifted Dan and me in equal portions after selling the store. Right now, I'm renting it to a co-worker and making a little profit.

"Also, I'm renting my car – which I bought from a friend with cash – another small profit. I won't need a car in Seoul since you have one. When necessary, I can use a taxi. I'll continue using my two credit cards for various items, including clothes, which I don't buy very often. I pay the total on my credit cards monthly. My PR firm has given me a corporate card for business expenses and the firm covers medical and life insurance for me.

"Oh, and I've managed to put some emergency funds into a savings account. I've also invested in my firm's 401K plan. So… that's it, that's my financial story."

Ki looked a little surprised, "Wow, you're as admirable with personal finances as you are with your work. I would like to do more if you'll let me. If you accept the idea that half of the tour income I'll receive is yours, you might be able to pay off your condo loan. I respect that it's important for you to have a good credit score by using your own credit cards. That's a good idea. We could set up a bank account in your name to cover the payments on those cards, plus cash for other items you want to buy."

I smiled at him and got tears in my eyes. I had been on my own for so long. "I love your kindness and generosity, Ki. I appreciate the way you want to take care of me. Thank you. We'll work it out as we go along." I put my hand on his cheek and kissed him. "I'm not a person who cares about material possessions beyond what I need. I admit that not having to worry about covering my budget would be a relief." I hadn't thought about this aspect of living with Ki.

I said, "By the way, when we go to California, I know you'll like my mom and brother as well as his family. His children are very cute, both under five. They'll love you! I've sent them YouTube links to some of the videos so they know how handsome and talented you are."

"It won't bother them that I'm Korean?" Ki asked.

"No, not at all. They're very open people. And, besides, you're perfect in every way." I kissed him. "Especially your lips, they're beyond perfect, they're 'perfectalicious.'"

I liked making Ki laugh.

One of the great things about Paris is that a couple can be affectionate in public and no one thinks anything of it. We couldn't do that in Seoul or in some places in the US. But, in that outdoor café, even though we were surrounded by people, and being watched by a bodyguard, we were in our own little world of love.

After lunch, both of us happened to put on our shades at the same time, then started laughing. We wandered through the streets of Paris, two disguised lovers with our bodyguard in tow and joked about being disguised runaways. We made an indulgent dash through the emerging artists showing at the Palais de Tokyo. Then, hopped a boat ride on the Seine.

Relaxing into the upper deck seats, I said, "This reminds me of a story one of my colleagues in LA told me years ago." Ki looked interested.

"Her friend, an American man, Brad, met a French woman while they were both traveling through Europe on a train. They were in their twenties and single. She lived in Paris. They began a conversation with each other and really enjoyed talking. Near sunset, they arrived in Barcelona and decided to hop off the train and sightsee around the city. The next morning, they were each headed home.

"Well, they ended up spending the whole night talking as they explored the city. They surprised themselves, being very open and revealing in their exchange on this moonlit night.

"Eventually, they began to feel a romantic connection. Near dawn, they found themselves on a little patch of grass near the beach with no one around and they made love.

"At sunrise, they had to hurry to the train station after waking up late. In their rush, they decided not to exchange phone numbers or addresses. They figured they'd forget about each other after getting back home to their daily lives."

Ki caught it, "Oh, that's going to be a mistake. Wait, was this pre-cell phones?"

"Yes, no phones! So, that was it. They both went back home.

"The American guy dated several women over the next few years. Then, his friends started getting married. He caved and married a woman, a longtime friend, that he didn't deeply love.

"The French woman had other relationships, too, but none, not one, had the spark she'd experienced with him during that one night. She didn't marry. As they got older, both of them realized that having the kind of psychologically intimate connection they experienced is rare. Very few people encounter the kind of intellectual and physical compatibility that they felt with each other that amazing evening."

Ki was listening to my every word. Finally, gazing into his beautiful, brown eyes, I said, "I am so thankful that you didn't continue ignoring me after we first met. I'm so glad that you took a chance on developing this relationship."

"So am I. It feels like it was the best decision I'll ever make." He kissed me. "You know, that's a compelling story. Is there more to it?"

"Oh, yes. In fact, this must be the reason I recalled it. Eventually, the two of them met again! Brad's investigative journalism career hadn't helped his marriage and they divorced about four years in. He searched for a job in Paris and purposely settled in the neighborhood where she had said she lived.

"After about six months, he spotted her two rows up on the ferry they were riding along the Seine. She was surprised and thrilled to see him. Part of her reawakened.

"She was living with an actor but things weren't good. She and Brad began spending time together and soon felt the same close connection they'd had in the beginning. My friend tells me that, eventually, they married and had children. They're still happy, years later."

"What an epic tale. I'm glad it came to you. Mara, you're a good storyteller."

At this point in our journey through the city, we had disembarked the boat in the 12th Arr. and were sitting on a bench surrounded by roses and playful sculptures in the Parc de Bercy.

Ki then said, "This is a very personal question and of course you don't have to answer if you don't want to, but are there any romantic relationships that you've had in the past that you regret ending, as happened in the story?"

I thought for a few seconds, then said, "No, I'd say each one ran its course and usually I learned something from it. But they ended when they should have. How about you?"

"I haven't had any good romantic relationships, nothing even ten percent of what we have. My sadness has been the fear that I wouldn't be able to find a woman who would love me and whom I could love."

I was surprised, "That's hard to believe, considering who you are and that millions of women love you."

"You're referring to fans when you say 'millions.' As you know, the company has a strict rule about avoiding involvements with fans or employees of the company. Beyond that, I haven't always been the person I am now.

"In K-pop, like rap, it's important to be a player. I tried that for a while a few years ago. It wasn't for me. But I've learned a lot about myself. There are things I've changed. I'm still working on it, but I hope that I can love you enough that you'll want to stay with me."

I felt a sudden sadness hearing Ki express concern that I might not want to stay. "Ki, I can't imagine not wanting to stay with you based on what we've experienced so far."

He went on, somewhat apologetically, "As I've mentioned before, I can get very caught up in the work – the creative process of writing lyrics, composing, the choreography, studio sessions, the management of the team, you know?"

He watched me intently as he spoke, "The stress and the psychology of it all is one of the reasons most of my other relationships ended. I'll do whatever I can to make you happy and keep you in my life." His tone was so sincere, "I hope you'll tell me if you're ever uncomfortable with me."

"I will, I promise. And will you do the same? That will be our promise to each other. We won't let small discomforts turn into a pattern."

His look of concern changed to one of relief, "Oh my God, what you said is so beautiful. Conflict resolution techniques are the way that the guys and I have been able to stay together for as long as we have.

"We try to have a meeting every week and discuss any problem that's going on in the group. We open up about things and try to find a solution."

I said, "This is a good idea for me because I can have difficulty bringing up a problem with someone I love. It's because I don't want to sound as though I'm criticizing that person. As I was growing up, my mother's sister used to make demeaning statements toward me or question what I wanted to do or was excited about. She always found something wrong with it.

"But I could never speak up about her comments because my mother always took her side and would be upset with me if I said anything that was considered disrespectful to an older person.

"All those years of training based on my mother's rules keeps me from speaking up with people I care about. With business people it's different, I have no problem. When there's any kind of disagreement, once I lay out the facts motivating my perspective, I find that most clients are open to new information and are agreeable. That's why my work doesn't stress me but personal relationships can."

Ki said, "I'm sorry that you had to deal with your aunt's attitude and demeaning remarks. That sounds hurtful and uncomfortable, especially with your mom taking her side. But I'm glad that you're open to using conflict resolution techniques.

"Still, in my experience, resolving conflicts in a romantic relationship between a man and a woman doesn't seem to be as easy as resolving conflicts between guys. What has your experience been?"

"What do you mean?" I asked.

"You mentioned before that you've learned something from each relationship you've had even though you didn't feel that it was worth keeping. I guess that's what I want to learn about. I'm always trying to figure out what makes a relationship work or not, and was there anything that made it worthwhile. So, I'm asking what has been good and bad in your relationships with men?"

I laughed a little, "This feels somewhat embarrassing, talking with you about my previous relationships. Do you really want to go there?"

"Yeah, I'm interested in everything about you and it seems that close relationships are an important part of that. Another reason I want to know about your likes and dislikes is that I don't want to lose you because I'm making some mistake that bothers you but I don't realize it. If I can prevent a problem by learning what bothered you in the past, that would be good."

"Oh, well, okay." My reply was halting. "Let me think through this out loud. Probably because I got along well with my dad and my brother, I expected respectful treatment from the boys I knew in my neighborhood and at school. My first boyfriend in high school lived just a couple of houses away from mine. I was 14. He was two years older and would come over on a regular basis to talk. A romance developed between us.

"Then, at some point, every couple months he would become angry about some small issue, would be quite mean about it, and I would break up with him. He would always apologize two or three times. In a few weeks, we would get back together. But the same occurrence would happen a month or so later. After a while, I wasn't interested in continuing with him.

"He left home to go to college when I was in my third year of high school. I had begun dating a different boy who was kinder, a basketball star. But when my ex-boyfriend came home from college during the holidays, he phoned me and asked if we could get together to talk about his college experiences.

"I said 'yes' since it was going to be a discussion between friends at that point. He came over and spent a couple of hours talking about what it was like being at the university. He was excited about what he was learning.

"At that time, I wasn't planning to go to college because my parents had not encouraged it, even though I was a good student. But my parents didn't have the money, and in my family, it just wasn't discussed. Additionally, they had done well by starting their own business and my brother was starting his home-building business. So, they didn't imagine a business degree was a necessity for becoming an entrepreneur.

"But, during our talk that day, my ex-boyfriend emphasized how many great scholarships are available and noted what a good writer I am. I can still remember that realization as I was listening to him, the fresh desire to attend college.

"Not that I wanted to attend the same school he did but I wanted to experience the excitement of learning at a higher level. After that, I studied more, improved my grades and landed a good scholarship.

"So, I would say that he helped to change my life even though he wasn't someone that I wanted to have an ongoing relationship with. Seems like we saw each other only a couple more times after that day."

"I'm fascinated." Ki said. "You didn't want a relationship with someone who angers easily or is mean to you but that person changed your life. What did you learn from the next boyfriend, the basketball star?"

"I can't believe we're talking about this." I still felt embarrassed going on. But Ki was looking at me with such expectation. "OK - the basketball star was easy to get along with but not intelligent enough. I realized I wanted someone as intelligent or more intelligent than I am… like you."

"Thanks for the compliment. I may be as intelligent but I doubt that I'm more intelligent than you. But did you date someone who was more intelligent while in college?"

I laughed at this point thinking back to the guy I dated in college. "Maybe he was more intelligent. He was a chemistry major and was president of a fraternity that was a lot of fun. So, besides working hard on studies for his good grades, he ran the frat and we went to a lot of parties. He was easy to get along with and fun, but he didn't have the depth of feeling that matched mine. You do."

Ki smiled, "Thank you. What about after college?"

At this point, I went on without hesitation as Ki seemed so intrigued.

"After college, I dated a corporate attorney. He's probably more intelligent than I am, was easy to get along with, and he had accomplished some extraordinary things in his life which made him interesting. He also had a depth of feeling and was fun to be with.

"But I didn't have enough sexual chemistry with him to want to continue the relationship. With you the chemistry is amazing. As we discussed before, it's very rare to find the kind of psychological closeness and exciting physical intimacy that we have."

I paused for a moment while he was thinking. Then added, "So, how *do* I love thee? Let me count the ways - you're handsome, you're sexy, you're brilliant, you're patient, kind and even-tempered, you're successful and generous, you have a great body and a beautiful face that I love, and you're in love with me."

Ki was smiling as he listened to my list of his attributes. "Wow," he laughed. "That's fantastic to hear. After removing the word handsome, all those attributes belong to you as well. You're amazingly sexy, brilliant, patient, kind, even-tempered, successful, have a great body and beautiful face. I'm deeply in love with you and you love me. I feel very lucky," He kissed me. "Very, very lucky to have you in my life."

I said, "Evidently, we're a good match."

After a moment of reflection, he said, "Do you mind if we continue this discussion a little more?"

"Okay."

"I have friends and you probably do too, who have married people that they weren't excited about, like the guy your friend knew. They just go through the motions without really being in love. I don't want that. I'm excited about you and deeply in love with you. But I don't know how you feel about marriage. Are you eager to be married?'"

I laughed, "No, I don't think that marriage vows, a marriage license or a ceremony will keep two people in love or together. To stay in love, I believe that people need to feel it, as we do now, plus be caring and considerate, share interests and values, have in-depth conversations and great sex.

"It's about intimacy, mutual respect and honesty in my opinion. And, I think it takes a few months of being together to know if those characteristics will continue in daily life."

He said, "Agreed! Do you want to get married at some point?"

"Yes, at some point, definitely before having children."

Then, before he could ask me another question, I said, "I'll tell you something that is more personal." I hesitated as he looked at me. "Although I had a certain amount of physical intimacy with the two boys I dated in high school and the fraternity guy I dated in college, I didn't have sexual intercourse with them.

"I was raised going to church each week and to be a 'good girl.' Plus, my brother talked to me about being careful and smart when in a relationship. But the main reason was that... this is going to sound silly ... I had the idea that I wanted to be a virgin when I got married." I looked down before looking at Ki, feeling a little embarrassed about my naivete when I was younger.

He said, "I appreciate that you're sharing this."

I continued, "When I was 14, my first year of high school, we had a presentation at a special assembly in the auditorium. The whole high school population attended to learn about how the joining of a man and a woman sexually is a bond that is sacred and shouldn't happen until marriage. It was very well presented by a male doctor and a female psychologist. High school presentations like that were popular then.

"In my school, most of the kids took it seriously and many of us signed a pledge that we would keep that promise. Even some younger celebrities in the US were saying the same thing at that time. So, it seemed important. Also, I didn't want to be one of those girls who had sex to get it over with. Or, as some would say, 'It's just sex.' It wasn't that way for me.

"After college, I realized that waiting until I was married was naïve because I might not get married for years. But my sexual encounter, with only one man before you – the attorney – was disappointing. As I mentioned before, he was interesting, fun, attractive, but the sexual chemistry wasn't there for me.

"I'd met him through friends. We began dating and eventually had sex. I didn't have an orgasm with him and, after a while, I ended the relationship. But we remained friends."

Ki looked at me with surprise, "So, when we made love last night, I was only the second man that you've had sex with? And, that was your first orgasm resulting from intercourse?"

Taking a deep breath, I looked at him, "Yes, you're the *only* man that I've experienced an orgasm with during intercourse... and with you, it was amazing. I loved it."

He looked at me for a couple seconds, then developed an irrepressible smile, "That makes me really happy. I mean, you're telling me that I gave you the 'sacred gift' that you've been waiting for since you were fourteen-years-old. No wonder you looked like a frightened little girl standing before me in the bedroom, trembling."

I said, "I felt a little that way, yes, and part of me was aware that I was risking my career. I had decided to trust you. But admittedly I wasn't certain you loved me."

"I do love you and our conversation today strengthens that love. This means a lot to me. I'm grateful that you answered my questions and shared such intimate details about your life. This is the most in-depth conversation I've ever had with anyone, man or woman. Is there anything you want to ask me about my past relationships?"

"Only if there's something you want to tell me. However, as long as no women come banging on our door in Seoul, yelling about how you told them you loved them, I think I'm okay for now." I said jokingly.

He laughed. "No, there will be no women at the door unless we've ordered take-out. Actually, before you, I've never told any woman that I love her because I haven't felt this feeling with anyone but you.

"But, Mara, I was hoping for it. I haven't even dated anyone during the last year. That's the reason I avoided you the first week after we met, I was confused. I wasn't sure about what I was feeling. Then, I realized that I wanted to learn more about you and see where it would lead. Thank God, I did."

At this point, a couple more hours had passed. We decided to Google a good bistro nearby. Far from the glamour of the city center now, we found a classic spot that featured natural wines and fresh oysters every Sunday, perfect.

My phone was filled with names of Parisian clubs LA friends had texted me. But, after dinner, we headed back to the hotel knowing the next day would be full speed ahead. In the car, I edited and sent a few ideal images to Seoul which I'd managed to take with Ki in silhouette as we floated by the Eiffel Tower.

Just a teaser for more from Paris since the camera crew had a major VLIVE shoot scheduled with the guys in the days ahead. It was a packed week.

We went to bed early and had another passionate night that included the sacred gift Ki was giving me. Again, it was beautiful. I felt fortunate that we were so in love with each other and so compatible – in every way I could imagine.

9 Back to Work

Early on Monday morning, we had a meeting with the BL6 team. When Ki and I walked into the room together, the guys each had a big smile for us along with a cake and flowers to celebrate our now official relationship. We both laughed and thanked them. We felt happy for their support and a little embarrassed because we imagined what they were thinking about our activities for the last couple of nights.

Bin said, "Now that you two have been together for a whole weekend, is the relationship still on? My relationships don't usually make it to Monday."

We all laughed and Ki said, "Yeah, I'm glad to say, it's still on."

After we each had a slice of cake and some tea, I gave them a couple of pages of information. As usual, I'd uploaded it to BestStars' in-house project management program so it was pushed to each of their phones.

This time, I included sound files for a few short, French language comments they could use in the TV and radio shows scheduled that afternoon. There would be an interpreter on each show but they appreciated the French options. So, this morning I'd invited our interpreter in to help them polish pronunciation.

Also, I ran through likely interview questions the producers shared, so the guys knew how to listen for keywords the hosts might use. They felt confident.

In Paris, we sold out the arena for two consecutive nights soon after we arrived. Expectations were high.

♥

During that week, I Skyped my mom and brother. I told them how during the last couple months, Ki and I had developed a serious relationship and decided to move in together. I told them I would be living with him in Seoul after the tour but would be back to visit them during the winter.

My brother, Dan, asked if Ki is good to me, I said, "Yes, he's very kind and thoughtful."

Dan said, "Don't tolerate anything less, Mara. You know celebrities concern me."

"And you know I've never been involved with one until now. Don't worry, Dan, he's a very caring person. You'll like him."

Mom said, "How will you adjust to living in Seoul, doesn't it get snowy there in winter? You've never liked that."

"I know, that will be an adjustment," I answered. "Ki suggested that I fly to California to visit the two of you and get some sun any time I want to, and whenever possible, he'll come with me."

Mom said, "How will you afford that, Mara?"

I told her, "Ki's offered to cover travel expenses. He doesn't want me to pay for anything while we're together. He's very generous. He even wants to pay off my mortgage because, in his view, it was my publicity work that doubled the number of concerts and boosted tour income."

She asked, "Your mortgage? Does he have that kind of money?"

"Yes, Mom, this band is very successful. Each of the band members is on track to be a multi-millionaire. Ki also owns a beautiful condo in one of the nicest areas of Seoul."

"Oh, my goodness. That's amazing! I didn't realize that, Mara," she seemed relieved.

Next, Mom asked if we were planning to get married.

"Maybe, eventually. Ki asked me what I would like to do. But, Mom, you know how I feel about marriage. I want to wait a few years. We know we both want children, so we'll be married before that happens."

Mom said, "Wow, sounds as though you two have discussed all the details. That's exciting!"

I then let them know I would introduce Ki to them through Skype during the week ahead. We agreed on an evening that would be best. Then, I asked a few questions about them and we ended our conversation with "I love you," as we usually do. By then, I felt Mom was pleased.

On Tuesday's Skype, they met Ki. Everything went well. As always, he was remarkable, relaxed and friendly. We talked for quite a while. He managed to quell my brother's protective skepticism. They liked him.

♥

During the week in Paris, BL6 was putting in long hours alternating press days with the social team's fan events. An arena check prompted added rehearsals to work through onsite issues in the choreography. Those went on right up to the night before the first concert.

Ki got home about ten, earlier than previous nights. I was in bed and had been reading. I put my book down when I heard him come in. Our busy schedules had kept us from any sex for a few days. Being a new couple, days felt like months.

Ki walked into the bedroom still sweaty from dance practice, his shirt was soaked. He smiled, "I hoped you'd be awake. I've been thinking about you all day." As he stood beside the bed, he took my hand and kissed my palm. "I want to make love to you. I'll take a shower and be right back."

The soaked shirt clinging to his chest made his nipples show through. That, and his tousled hair made him look even sexier than usual. I said, "Let's do it now… shower after."

Considering his Korean tradition for cleanliness, I knew this would be a dilemma. I wasn't surprised when he said. "But, I'm sweaty. I'll get you dirty."

I responded in a soft voice, "I want you to get me dirty. I want to feel your moist skin against me." That said, I threw off the sheet I was under, exposing my nude body, then said, "But, the choice is yours."

At this point in our relationship, Ki had seen me naked every night, but in this moment, he was out of his clothes and on top of me in a matter of seconds – cleanliness be damned.

Feeling his warm body against mine, my heart and pulse quickened. I automatically took in a deep breath of excitement. We were both breathing harder. His kisses were passionate, loving, hungry. My every nerve was responding. He kissed my lips and body. My pulse and voice reacted to every point of contact. My body was his.

It took only a few thrusts for both of us to have an amazing orgasm. He always made sure that I started to climax first.

The pleasure was intense, like being in another dimension. In those moments, we forgot everything else. Only our feelings and impulses existed. Afterward, we lay together, in silence, with tremors of excitement still pulsing through us.

In a few minutes, looking at me with love in his eyes, Ki said, "That was *unbelievable*. You create feelings in me that I've never even had before. I'm so in love with you."

"It was beautiful," I sighed. "I'm glad I can make you feel so good. When you make love to me, it's like I'm floating somewhere beyond time and place. Nothing else matters."

As he moved onto his back, he said, "Floating beyond time and place. I love that description."

I rolled toward him onto my stomach, slid my arm across his waist and licked his nipples. He laughed as though he was being tickled. I said, "You taste and smell good when you sweat. I love your body, sweaty or showered."

He said, "Let's take a shower together and do it again, just for the sake of comparison, like a scientific experiment."

"Ok, Professor." We showered, were playful and laughed as we soaped each other from top to bottom. Then we rinsed each other's bodies, dried off and made love a second time. It was transporting and fun.

The next morning, opening day of the two-night Paris run, Ki was off early to prep with BL6. But he took time before they left for the sound check to bring lunch for both of us and two dozen red roses.

With the flowers was a beautiful card in which he had written, "To Mara, the love of my life. May we often float beyond time and place. All my love, Ki"

I was so touched by his thoughtfulness, especially on such a busy day, that I got tears in my eyes. I held him, then looked at his stunning face for a few seconds, "Thank you for loving me. I love you with every fiber of my being."

♥

Now that Ki and I would be living together, I wanted to add to my eveningwear. I had only one short satin robe with me because it was easy to pack. That afternoon, I visited a lingerie shop and bought two beautiful satin mid-thigh length robes.

One was black with three large long-stemmed flowers on it composed of green leaves and petals in orange, yellow and red, two in the front and one up the back. The second robe was white with a see-through lace front from the shoulders to the waist, front and back, plus ruffled lace cuffs finishing the three-quarter length sleeves. I like light-weight robes because the belt is easy to untie and the robe slides off. Great for love-making.

I also bought three sets of thongs with snaps on the sides, one in red, one black and one white. I selected matching bras in satin lace. These purchases were expensive, but I wanted to look as sexy as I felt and for Ki to enjoy what I was wearing in the evenings. I felt it was a worthwhile investment.

The first time I wore the lacy white satin robe, Ki loved it. As soon as he saw me, he said, "You look beautiful, like an angel, a very sexy angel." He kissed me as he untied the belt and let the robe drop to the floor. Then he picked me up, laid me on the bed, undressed and made love to me. His reaction seemed almost compulsive. That's what I hoped would happen.

A few nights later, I wore the black robe with flowers. He loved it too and said the dark color made me look mischievous which also turned him on and lead to more love-making. Ki is a man who is not only strong, but also sensitive, aware of his feelings and mine. I adore that about him.

♥

Both concerts in Paris were *fire* and equally well-reviewed.

After the ageless City of Lights where our lives changed, we were off to London and, later, Berlin. More interviews, streamlining of choreography and the band's one liners. We were in a great rhythm for the string of sold-out nights.

While there, I was lining up magazine shoots and interviews for the Osaka and Seoul concerts that would finish this year's tour. San-A and the whole social team were a huge help in sharing contacts who'd already provided great coverage on earlier tours, particularly in Japan.

We went to Osaka first, where it felt like the team, the band, the press, the social fam, all of us just clicked. Items on the schedule fell like dominos in some epic viral TikTok.

Finally, we were in Seoul. We had about four days before the concerts.

The airport arrival was the craziest yet. It was as if every fan in the country had found their way to our terminal to welcome BL6 home. I thought of Chicago and my talk with the security guard about the crowd there not having that edge of wild tension. The Incheon International Airport, packed with stans, must have been peppered with sasaengs.

By the time we arrived at Ki's condo, it felt like a triumph. After unlocking the door and removing our shoes to enter, he swept me up, literally, off my feet and carried me inside, proclaiming, "Welcome home, Babe. I hope you like it."

I was giggling through every moment of his romantic gesture. I glanced across the open loft design and easily matched his enthusiasm, "I *love* it!" He put me down and I took a few moments to look around more thoroughly. "You've made beautiful choices. I love the colors and the furniture. The paintings are extraordinary."

I turned to face him, "You called me babe. You haven't done that before."

He grinned, "You *are* a babe, a beautiful, sexy babe... that I love. In Korean, 'jagi' is a term of endearment, but I like to speak English with you and for you, 'babe' seems to fit. I think it may be an American expression."

I put my arms around him, "I like it."

The condo was on the top floor of the large complex. It was spacious and had lots of windows and natural light. It looked newly built with a cream-colored ondol (heated floor) and white furniture that was contemporary with soft, comfy cushions. The beautiful works of art added color.

The kitchen had white cabinets and walls of pale buttercup yellow, granite counter-tops with the look of marble, and stainless-steel appliances. There were two good-sized bedrooms and two bathrooms, one in our bedroom and one for guests.

Ki opened the refrigerator and got a beer. He held the door open and asked, "Would you like something?"

I saw that the fridge was fully stocked with groceries and bottled drinks. I said, "Is there a lemonade? Who bought all the groceries?"

Ki handed me a lemonade and said, "About a year ago, I hired a wonderful older woman who cleans, buys groceries and sometimes cooks for me. You'll like her, Soo-Jung. She's very kind."

"Wow! That's great." Suddenly, I realized that I wouldn't have to spend much time cleaning.

Ki brought in our luggage and we unpacked in the master bedroom which had white walls, navy-blue drapes and a matching comforter on the queen-sized bed.

The head of the bed was against the north wall. On the west wall were windows and the south wall had a bathroom with shower. Beyond the bathroom were long closets where Ki's clothes filled half the space with room for my clothes in the other half. Two dressers stood along the east wall and entrance door, which had a full-length mirror facing the bed. Most of the space along the walls had bookshelves filled with Ki's collection.

The second bedroom was similar but without the bathroom, which was off the alcove to that part of the condo and had a tub with a shower above it. The second bedroom closet was stuffed with more of Ki's clothes plus a separate wardrobe rack beyond the closet.

I said, "I always wondered where you guys keep all the clothes you wear for photoshoots, videos, vacations, all the events. You each must have a thousand different outfits."

He answered, "We do have a lot of clothes. Anything for work is custom made for us. The company pays for everything we wear on professional shoots, even company-filmed vacations.

"They warehouse most of those clothes but we get links to a site showing numbered photos of them in case we want to wear something for a personal event. A staff member delivers it. Also, this condo building has storage units on the bottom floor, so some of my items are there, besides what I have here in my place."

"That's extraordinary!" Even as a PR pro, I was amazed.

Ki shrugged. "I know. But doing so many shoots and public appearances requires it. Plus, companies that we partner with send clothes for each member and magazines that we do a shoot for usually provide our wardrobe because they want a certain look. Once in a while, it's gifted to us."

As we unpacked, he said, "By the way, if you have any changes you want to make to the décor here in the condo, feel free to do so. I want you to feel at home here, Mara."

He stopped what he was doing, came to me and put his arms around my waist. "I'm so glad you're here with me. I still can't believe it sometimes." He kissed me.

"I'm glad, too, Ki. I love being with you. And as for the décor, I like all your choices. If I think of something to add, it will be minor."

Later that evening, as we ate delivery pizza and a salad I made., I did think of a couple of things. I mentioned to Ki that I'd like to bring in two or three large plants for greenery. He liked the idea. I said I would get instructions from the nurseryman on which ones would be best for the light in the condo. Also, I thought I would like to add some pillows for the sofa that pick-up the colors in the paintings. Ki said that would look great. Those were my only changes.

The next day while Ki was working, his housekeeper, Soo-Jung, stopped by to meet me during the afternoon. She is a lovely, white-haired grandmother with plenty of stamina. She offered to cook a "welcome home" Korean dinner, Ki's favorite, Bulgogi.

It has thinly sliced beef with a smoky sweet flavoring, she added garlic and sliced onions, plus lettuce wraps. Also, she made her special version of Japchae – stir-fried noodles with mushrooms, and a bit of soy sauce. Kimchee was the side dish, spicy fermented vegetables. We talked as she was cooking. I wrote down her recipe for Japchae. Because it wasn't complicated, I thought I'd make it for dinner some nights.

Soo-Jung told me that she thought very highly of Ki and said he is the kindest person she had ever worked for. She shared stories about her family and the reasons she loves Seoul. She also asked about my life. I thoroughly enjoyed our conversation.

All the cooking was finished around 5:00 and Ki arrived home soon after to a condo filled with the aromas of his favorite meal. He was delighted. We both loved our first delicious Korean dinner that night, together in our home.

I liked living in the Hannam neighborhood where so many other celebrities had moved. With Soo-Jung's help, I not only didn't have to clean much but I also cooked very little which I was happy about. My work hours were long and we were surrounded by great restaurants with menus for delivery. Some nights, we ordered our favorites and other nights, I made American recipes that we both like.

I usually prefer vegetarian meals, often making mixed steamed vegetables with beans and brown rice or potatoes for both of us. And, for Ki, I cook some beef, chicken or pork to add to his plate. With dinner, we usually have a salad of greens.

Plus, I regularly make Soo-Jung's Japchae recipe and keep a large jar of kimchee in the fridge as a side dish. Ki often tells me how much he appreciates my accommodating his food choices. I'm happy learning the more classic Korean dishes, meat or not. Seoul is my new home.

After dinner, Ki usually helps clear the table, fill the dishwasher and clean the kitchen. A couple nights a week, he has a Korean dinner with his BL6 brothers to have some casual time with them. We both know that's important. I always have plenty of work to do. Also, I enjoy the pleasure of lying in bed by myself, relaxing and reading a book.

One evening while we were having dinner, Ki said, "I was thinking today about how I used to dread coming to this condo. I would work in my office at BestStars until I was exhausted, barely able to stay awake. Then, I would come here, take a shower and fall into bed. The place felt empty and lonely. Now, with you, I'm eager to be here. It's warm and full of loving energy, a real home. I knew you were extraordinary, Mara, but I didn't imagine all the beautiful things you would do just to make me happy. I'm so grateful." He gazed at me for a few moments.

I listened closely to his comments as I looked at his handsome face, "That's beautiful, Ki. Thank you."

♥

After living together a few days, a rare thing happened when we were sleeping, I woke up, gasping for breath, loudly enough that it woke Ki.

He murmured, "What's wrong? Are you OK?"

I said, "Oh, I'm sorry I woke you. Just a dream. The same frightening dream that I've had many times. It doesn't happen very often.

Ki asked, "What dream is it? It must be bad if it woke you like that."

"It's a dream that someone is going to stab me. I can't see who it is because they're behind me, but I can feel them coming closer."

"That's terrible. How often does it happen?"

"Only once every five or six months. It doesn't seem to be linked to stress or anything that I can think of. I guess it's just an irrational fear that's in my subconscious. I've never known what it's about. I'm okay now. Thanks for your concern. Let's go back to sleep."

♥

Ki, Bin and JJ had invited their families to the first of the two Seoul concerts. Ki and I decided to have a party at our condo afterward so the parents could chat with each other.

He said that we should have it catered to make it easy. One evening he and I made a playlist and selected foods we wanted the catering company to supply. They would also bring floral bouquets for the table, plates, napkin-wrapped silverware, and would send two waiters along.

The night before the first concert in Seoul, Ki got in late. He dropped onto the sofa next to me. He had eaten dinner with the boys. I had just changed into my robe. I hugged him and said, "It seems you've been stressed this week."

He looked at me apologetically, then kissed me. "Yeah, we're in Seoul. I feel the concerts have to be perfect, especially knowing my family, Bin and JJ's families will be in the audience for the first night. Plus, we're hosting the party afterward. You'll be spending an evening and morning with my parents for the first time. It feels like a lot of extra pressure. I haven't been sleeping very well. I hope I haven't been difficult to be with."

"No, only quiet, lost in your thoughts and concerns. You know you can talk to me about anything at any time."

He kissed me and said, "I know. I can be that way, I'm sorry. I have to work on that."

"I thought of something special that might help you relax and sleep better tonight.

He smiled at me, "Why do you have that mischievous look on your face?"

"Because it's something that we do in bed that requires being nude and includes these." I held up four wide red satin ribbons, each about two feet long. "Do you want to try it?"

Ki realized what I was talking about and laughed, "Who are you?" he asked.

I continued, "There's one rule: After we start, you can't talk or... move."

"Oh, I don't know if I can do that, but I'll try." We went into the bedroom. As I gently kissed him, I unbuttoned his shirt and took it off. He removed the rest of his clothes.

"Lie down and close your eyes. This is an ancient meditation."

Ki said, "I'll bet."

I said, "Now, we stop talking. With your eyes closed, breathe deeply."

I loosely tied his wrists to the headboard and ankles to the footer of our bed. Then, I removed my robe, quickly pulled my hair back into a bun so it wouldn't tickle him and started lovingly kissing his lips, his eyelids, ears, licking that perfect spot on his neck.

I gently sucked his nipples and ran my tongue around their soft edges, then slowly slid my tongue over his abs. I moved further down and began giving him as much oral pleasure as I knew how. I wanted him to give up control and the concerns that he was feeling, give nothing and just receive.

His breathing and the sounds he was making, some I'd never heard him make before, told me I was succeeding. Afterward, I removed the ribbons and pulled his now-relaxed arms to his sides, covered us with a sheet and snuggled beside him with my arm across his waist.

He whispered, "That was pure pleasure. I can't even talk…or move."

I whispered, "No need to do anything, sweetheart, just relax and sleep." We both slept very well that night; and the next day, we felt great.

♥

The first night of the concert was astonishing! It's true what they say about hometown crowds, all over the world. The three sets of parents attended and loved the performance. We all met afterward at our condo. The catering company did an excellent job, the food and service were exquisite.

There were twenty of us: All the BL6 members, six parents, three siblings of the members, two managers, including Manager Choi, two BL6 staff and me. The food filled the buffet and dining room table. We had wine, beer and traditional Korean Cheongju, a liquor distilled from steamed rice that reminded me of sake.

The two waiters replenished the table and guests' drinks as needed. Ki and I were so happy with the results. Everyone seemed to enjoy being there and chatting with each other. The conversations and laughter were constant during the evening.

Manager Choi gave a beautifully-worded toast to the boys, to the parents for raising such outstanding young men, to Ki and me regarding our new relationship and for bringing everyone together.

I talked with Ki's parents and sister off and on throughout the evening for the first time since our Skype conversation. I felt comfortable with them and they seemed to like me. At the end of dinner, the waiters put the remaining food in the fridge and took the dishes and silverware with them.

Ki's family spent the night in our extra bedroom, where Ki had added a special sleeping cot for his sister. The other parents spent the night with Bin and JJ.

The next day, Ki and I had breakfast with his family at the condo. The conversation was easy. Later, security drove us to the Hangaram Arts Museum for a private tour that Ki had arranged through his junior associates' membership.

We enjoyed the amazing works, strolling the galleries, talking along the way. We had lunch in a private second-floor room at a nearby restaurant. It overlooked a park with trees shimmering in Fall crimson, oranges and gold.

After the ride back to our condo, Ki had to go to work preparing for the second concert. His family left for their drive home, thanking us for what they described as "an outstanding, joyful experience." That summed my description, too. It was perfect and I felt so glad they enjoyed our time together.

A couple of days later, we received a lovely card by mail. Ki's mother wrote in Korean:

Dear Son and Mara,

Thank you for including us at the concert and your lovely party. We thoroughly enjoyed talking with the two of you as well as the band members, their parents and other guests. You both created a wonderful experience. The concert was amazing! We are so proud of both of you for making BL6 such an extraordinary success during this tour.

Ki, we are happy for your outstanding leadership ability of BL6. We can see that the boys think highly of you as does Hyun-Tae. It's clear that you are doing an excellent job managing the team. And, Mara, Manager Choi and the boys told us what extraordinary work you did with the publicity. Congratulations to both of you on such outstanding accomplishments and success.

Ki, we are very pleased that you and Mara are happy together. It was a pleasure talking with each of you. We look forward to a visit from you whenever you have time.

With love,
Mom and Dad

We were delighted with their kind comments.

♥

The day after the second concert in Seoul, the last concert of the tour, BestStars had an elaborate dinner party for everyone in the private room of an elegant Michelin Star restaurant called Bicena, with dizzying views of the city. It's on the 81st floor of Korea's tallest building, the Lotte World Tower.

The BestStars CEO, other executives, managers, BL6, staff and others were all there. Everyone was pleased that the group had so much success on this tour and the company chose to honor them.

During his speech that night, Manager Choi said, "I want to give Ms. Jansen credit for doing a great job with the publicity in each city. Her work boosted our great BestStars social team, helped to double our concerts and significantly increased profits for this tour. We are honored that she will continue as our publicity manager." I was thrilled to hear Hyun-Tae's praise and delighted with the bonus check the company deposited in my account.

As Manager Choi spoke, everyone looked in my direction and applauded. Ki was beaming with happiness. While they were applauding, the members of BL6 stood, then everyone did.

It felt for a few seconds like time stopped. It seemed my heart was being seen, doing the work that I'm supposed to do in life, helping deserving artists to gain greater success with less stress. I smiled, stood and bowed in deep gratitude.

The next day, Ki brought me a beautiful little rose-red box. Inside was a necklace with two intertwined outlines of hearts in gold. In tiny English letters he had the jeweler engrave Mara on the back of one heart and Ki on the back of the other. I was so pleased by this delicate gift.

I hugged Ki, "You are so thoughtful and loving. You're the joy of my life."

He smiled, kissed me, and fastened the necklace, then gazed at me, "It picks up the beauty of your golden hair."

♥

Within a week, BestStars had an assignment for me. They had a group of younger boys, teens, who were starting to plan their first tour in Korea, Japan and China. This kept me busy for the next few months as China was an entirely new market for me.

I received some guidance by the BestStars team which helped tremendously. My consulting firm in LA also had regular work for me, either in Asia or in California, during which I would travel to LA to work for a few days. I stayed busy as we all prepared for the next world tour.

Also, I took advanced Korean language classes where I met some ex-pats from the US who were fun to socialize with. And, through my yoga class, I met some Korean women that

I connected with and enjoyed. Ki worked a lot on writing and composing new music. But now, he did more of it at home than at his office. As he and BestStars' producers began laying down new tracks, he and BL6 started fresh choreography rehearsals.

♥

One night after dinner, we were working on our individual projects while sitting in bed. Ki said, "I feel I should tell you that I revealed a little about our sex life to Bin today."

"You did? Why?" I said as calmly as possible, although I cringed at the thought. I knew, because they were the closest in age, that he and Bin talked more than he did with the other members of the team. Still, I was concerned about what he had revealed.

Ki said, "He was curious about our relationship after seeing us together at the parties. It's hard for him to believe that we get along so well. Like me, before I met you, he hasn't had good relationships with women. It started when Bin said, 'Come on, Ki, this is great for now but be real with me, and with yourself, man. I mean, can you really keep up this sugary sweet exchange we see between you two?' You know how he is."

Ki told him, "Not if it's forced, no. But, Bin, it isn't. It's easy. In fact, easier! It's easier being like this, like I am with Mara, than arguing and being fought with and thinking that's all there is to love.

"Hey, I never *expected* a love like this, but I did dream about it. And now that it's here, I see - this *is* possible. I mean, Mara is so good to me. This is a love that makes me only, ever, want to express kindness to her, the right words for her and a level head for the choices we'll make in building our future."

Ki continued, "Bin said, 'Well, time will tell. I'll wait and see how this turns out. For now, I'm happy for you, bro. Tell me - if I'm being too intrusive - with all this kindness, is the sex also good?'
Ki then said to me, "I'm so happy about our relationship that I couldn't resist telling him a couple of things." Ki was smiling as though this meant a lot to him.

"And, what were the couple of things?" I was beginning to feel more anxious.

He went on, "In my defense, I'll say that I've shared confidential information with Bin before and he hasn't repeated it as far as I know. I feel as though I can trust him."

"Okay, that's good, but what did you tell him," I asked again, still managing a tranquil tone.

"I told him that you're so responsive to my touch and my needs, that you've never said no when I want to make love to you, that you initiate sex almost as often as I do. It means so much to me that you respond like that. I'm like a different person compared to my life before you were in it.

"And, I explained to him that it's not only the sex but also the fact that you're interested in the books I read and that we both love art, architecture, and nature. You don't complain about the time I spend with the team or writing lyrics. I've never been this close to anyone. I've never had anyone who understands and accepts me the way you do."

As he spoke, he looked at me with such admiration and love in his eyes that my heart melted my concerns. I thought about how I had told my best friend about our sex life for the same reason, because I was so happy about it.

I said, "What you're saying is beautiful. I understand. In fact, I told Bree how good we are with each other... in every area."

Ki continued, "And, another reason I told him is that I want him to know it's possible to have the kind of relationship we do. I want him to find a woman who truly loves him. I want that for all the guys."

"I know, me too." I kissed him as I realized again what a caring person he is.

And so, we began the next phase of our lives together in Seoul, being close to our BL6 brothers and their friends, seeing Ki's family as often as we could. We added new friends, some Korean and some American, to our guestlists at home or we visited theirs. We rarely went to restaurants but had frequent dinners together, filled with good food, wine, conversation and fun.

When a problem between Ki and me arose, we worked it out as soon as possible and as calmly and considerately as possible. There were times when one or the other of us had to accept something we didn't necessarily like. But we understood from the beginning that compromise is part of any good relationship.

Most of the time we got along well just by being thoughtful and loving, remembering to value our relationship beyond daily stresses.

Our visits increased with Ki's family. They liked me and I enjoyed them. His mom is a little bit formal, an intelligent woman with her own business. We took his sister out for lunch and shopping a few times, had some great conversations with her about her life, what she likes doing, and what she wants to do in the future. Both of Ki's parents asked me about living in the US and they shared how they grew up and what they enjoy about living in Korea.

During one visit, Ki's mom seemed to feel particularly accepting of our relationship – maybe she'd decided we were going to last – and she broke with her normal reserve to explain to me how worried she was about him when he was a teen.

She said, "I can see now that Ki had a destiny that he was compelled to fulfill. Back then, we felt as though we were losing our wonderful son. We didn't know what to do and I know I made mistakes out of fear."

Hearing her words from the kitchen, Ki joined us, sat down on the sofa next to her and said, "Mom, you've never told me that."

She said, "I was afraid that if I brought it up, we would both become angry again."

Ki then put his arm around her shoulders. He said, "It's better now, right?"

She said, "Yes, much better. I'm very proud of you. You've become an extraordinary man. Back then, I didn't understand any of it. I regret some of my words and actions."

Ki got tears in his eyes, "Thanks, mom, hearing you say that means a great deal to me. I regret disappointing you and dad at that time. I know that I caused concerns for you both."

That conversation helped him have more understanding and compassion for his mom. I was surprised when he gave me credit for helping her to open-up about the past.

10 *Thanksgiving in California*

During November, a few days before Thanksgiving, we flew to California for the holiday to visit my brother, his family and my mom, Jane. We didn't bring a bodyguard, Ki donned his bucket hat/shades combo, plus the authentic beard/mustache pairing. Somehow, he looked even sexier than usual.

Once we were seated on the plane, I leaned toward him, whispering in my most alluring tone, "So glad I was seated next to you, Roberto, you're hot."

Ki found this very funny. We both laughed off and on during the flight because I couldn't resist staying in character and peppering our airtime with silly, sexy comments. Before we arrived at Dan's house, "Roberto" was removed and returned to what we were now calling 'the beard box.'

Ki enjoyed being with my family - talking with Dan about his work and with Selena about her ideas for improving their home. Plus, he had a couple of long chats with my mom, looking through family photo albums and listening to her stories about my brother and me. And, he must have played for over an hour with my niece and nephew.

My whole family liked him. Who wouldn't?! He's confident, charming, considerate, patient, sincere and a good listener. Plus, they could easily see that he loves me. Because he's used to people watching him, he had no qualms about putting his arm around me when others were in the room.

Thanksgiving was a special day. While we three women – Selena, my mom and I – were in the kitchen preparing the meal, Ki came into the room and asked if he could do anything to help. My mom said, "Ki, do you cook?"

He smiled and said, "With guidance I can cut vegetables, I can lift heavy pots and pans filled with food, and I've recently learned to make coffee in an electric coffee pot."

Through laughter, mom said, "Quite a resumé! Well, it's a start."

My nephew, Teddy, who had turned five that month, was sitting at the kitchen table. He said, "Ki, do you love my Aunt Mara?"

Selena and mom both looked toward Teddy; and Selena said, "Teddy, that's what's called a personal question and we don't ask grown-ups questions like that."

Ki leaned toward Teddy's sweet little face and said, "Yes, I do." I walked to Ki and put my arm around him.

Teddy went on, "She's pretty and she's nice, too."

"Yes, she is," Ki said. "I'm very lucky that she loves me."

Teddy responded with a grin, "I think you should kiss her."

Selena and Mom said, "Teddy!"

Ki smiled, "Teddy, I think that's a good idea. I'll ask her if it's okay. It's always good to ask.

"Mara, may I kiss you?"

I said, "Yes, you may."

Putting his arm around me, Ki then gave me a sweet kiss, lasting just long enough for a five-year-old's viewing. Afterward, we both looked at Teddy.

With a thumbs-up, he said, "That was a good one!"

Mom and Selena also had watched. After we all laughed at Teddy's response, Mom said, "That was lovely." Selena said, "Very romantic."

Before the family sat down for dinner, Ki showed Dan his camera. He even had Dan take some video of the table with everyone beginning to gather for the meal.

We all sat down and shared words of gratitude. Then, the feasting, the conversations, and the laughter began. My family took turns telling Ki funny stories from holidays gone by and he shared some Korean holiday traditions and family stories peppered with tales of life with the band.

After dinner, while everyone was still at the table, Ki stood, giving Dan a nod to start recording.

"I would like to take a few moments to say something. Spending time with each of you has been a beautiful experience for me. Thank you for being so welcoming and kind. It's my honor to visit Mara's family during this special holiday. It's also my honor and blessing to receive the love of this extraordinary woman."

Ki pushed his chair back and asked me if I would push my chair back from the table as well. He then got down on one knee before me. Suddenly, my pulse quickened, my hand automatically took its place over my heart. I focused on Ki's beautiful face and eyes.

With a glowing smile, he said, "Mara, I hope you will accept this token of my love for you with a proposal that whenever you are ready, we will be married. I know you don't like flashy jewelry, so I chose this ring that perhaps you will accept and enjoy." Ki opened a little box containing an emerald cut diamond, set in a delicate band of intertwined gold.

Tears welled up in my eyes, my hands were shaking, "Ki, this is beautiful. Of course, I accept your proposal and I will wear this ring with honor and love in my heart for our wonderful relationship. Thank you. I love you so very much."
Ki put the ring on my finger, a perfect fit! We stood, embraced and kissed each other.

My family applauded and all talked at once, saying how lovely our statements were and how they wish us a great deal of happiness. And, Dan got it all on Ki's camera.

I found out later that during the afternoon, Ki had told my brother and mom that he planned to propose to me and asked for their blessing.

My mom said, "I can see that the two of you are happy together. You have my blessing."

Dan followed with, "Ki, from what I can tell since we've known you, I believe you'll be very good to Mara. Thank you for asking us." They shook hands and mom gave Ki a hug.

It was a magical day, one I'll *never* forget.

Two days after Thanksgiving, we flew back to Seoul. Having Ki with me and my family made the holiday extraordinary, especially with the engagement.

He has such generosity and style. It wasn't until later that I learned how marriage proposals don't typically work that way in Korea. Their traditions are different. So, it meant even more to realize Ki had studied "proposals in US culture" and understood how important that could be to me and my family. He amazes me.

We hoped to go back at Christmas or soon after. Also, my California PR firm wanted me to do some work with them in LA in March, so that would be another trip, this time paid for by my company, with a week of sunlight and good friends. I could see my mom and brother again while there. In general, I Skype with them every week or so.

Plus, I stay in touch with Bree. She returned to Seoul in December for two weeks to further the consulting work she'd started last year, so we were able to share several dinners with her at our condo. She met Ki for the first time and loved his kindness and everything about him, really. She said to me privately, "Mara, he adores you! You found a good man. I'm so glad for both of you."

♥

So far, we've managed to keep our relationship a secret from the press. It helps that we don't go out to restaurants or clubs much, and when we do, we're usually part of a group, always in a private room. We go to art galleries and museums on private days and parks during off hours but no one bothers us. Our disguises – yes, I've developed one too – cover our hair, and Ki wears his "Roberto" beard so he's harder to spot.

Because Ki works long hours at home writing and composing, he's added production equipment in the guest bedroom. I continue to do my publicity work. My assignment from BestStars with the new, younger boy band keeps me busy during the work week at home. The view of

Seoul from our condo is infinitely fascinating. It's like living in the tree tops.

I'm loving my autonomy inside this life and I'm content for Ki and me to have whatever time we can together. The BL6 members say he's happier, more productive and less stressed now.

For that reason, they say that they don't mind him spending more time at home. They tell me that he's a better leader as a result. They still have conflict resolution meetings weekly, with each one opening-up about any frustrations, needs or concerns.

They train regularly, do photo shoots or advertisements for various companies and products, and generate a huge amount of content for social channels.

Every week, Ki makes a point of asking each member what, if anything, he can do for them. Besides that, he has dinner with them a couple times a week. Ki and I still manage long, interesting conversations, usually on weekends or our rare nights off during the week. And the passion? That's 24/7!

We're as close as ever.

Sandy N. Olson

K-pop Secret Love

11 *Surprises*

We didn't go back to California for Christmas because BestStars had booked a live performance for BL6 on a major TV network in Seoul. The show was a gem. Afterward, we all had dinner with friends at the network.

Since December 25th is a public holiday in South Korea, I also enjoyed a long Christmas Skype with my family (managing the 17-hour time difference).

On New Year's Eve, Bin had a dinner party with all the BL6 members, family and friends. His family hosted with about fifty guests. Both nights were fun and made the season festive for me with lots of warm conversations.

♥

One night in early January, after a couple weeks of Ki working long hours every day while writing lyrics for the new album, he came to bed late. I had just come out of the shower, gotten into bed and was adjusting my covers when I realized he was on his side, propped up on his elbow, staring at me.

I was amused, "Why are you looking at me so intently?"

Without changing his concerned expression, he responded, "I'm realizing that I'm not doing enough for you."

"What?!" my eyes softened. "I don't feel that way."

Unphased by my comment, he continued, "I don't want to have my work take over my life as it has during the last couple weeks. Those are my old habits and they aren't good for us.

"You're the most important part of my world, Mara. I'm realizing tonight that I've been neglecting you. I don't want to do that. I love you too much to continue this workaholic lifestyle. I fall into that habit without thinking. I've got to change it - I'm *going* to change it. You left your country, your family, friends, and your home – in sunny LA – to live with me in this wintry, dark city where you're a foreigner."

I started to say something comforting to him but he put his finger on my lips.

"I was thinking that we could take a few days off later this month and fly to LA, rent a house in Malibu, one with a private beach, and walk in the sun. You could visit your friends, and we'll go to San Francisco to see your family for a couple days. Would you like that?"

My jaw dropped! I couldn't believe what he was offering! Delighted, I threw my arms around him, accidentally pushing him onto his back while saying, "Oh, Ki, that's a beautiful idea! I love it! Can we really do that? I didn't think you had time to get away."

He started laughing at my overjoyed reaction, "I think Hyun-Tae will give time off since we had such success with the tour. I'll ask him tomorrow. I'm going to talk with the boys first about starting to write their own songs for the next album. We could each do some of that during our time away. I'll pitch it to Hyun-Tae as a 'working' vacation."

The next day, Ki talked with the other members and later with Manager Choi who agreed to give all the guys a week off during January with the idea that they would return with new songs or at least with new ideas and maybe the beginnings of new lyrics and music. Everyone was excited about the possibilities.

I checked on LA's extended weather forecast and it looked good for the last week of January. So, I booked flights through our BestStars travel agent. We rented a vacation house on the beach. I Skyped my brother, mom and Bree to let them know. They were delighted.

It was oddly thrilling to text friends knowing I could be seeing them in a few days.

> HNY! 🍸 Cocktails Thursday?

Wut? For real?! YES!!

Top of the list was Bree. We planned an evening at her house. I also hit up a few good friends I'd missed the last time I was home. We still had to keep our relationship a secret from most people, so I couldn't tell my friends that we were together. It didn't trouble me but it did involve some thought.

We arrived in LA on a Saturday afternoon, rented a car and headed to the vacation house. It did not disappoint!

We could see and hear the Pacific surf from inside the house. It was gorgeous, with the beach off the deck and the ocean a few feet away. The deck had plush wicker chairs and a little breakfast table plus – steam rising from a bubbling hot tub.

We had our first dinner outside that evening, ordering salmon, steamed cauliflower and farm-to-table salads from a nearby restaurant. Ki started a fire in the deck's firepit and there was a heat lamp to turn on as the evening cooled down. After dinner, we shared the rest of the sauvignon blanc in the hot tub, talking, laughing and watching the sunset. It was heaven.

Ki said, "I haven't been this relaxed for a while."

I kissed him and felt so much love for him. "You made this happen. This is a beautiful gift to us both. It's our belated engagement honeymoon."

That night, we stayed in the hot tub till the stars were shining in the dark velvet sky. We took a shower together, got into bed and made sweet, magical love under the stars shining through the bedroom skylight.

The way Ki moved on top of me was like the rhythm of the ocean and, unconsciously, I opened my arms outward on the bed, completely offering myself to him. He whispered, "When you do that, it makes me want to devour you."

I said, "You can, I'm yours."

The next day, Sunday, we walked along the beach after breakfast. Because we didn't have a bodyguard with us, Ki went as "Roberto" plus the bucket hat and sunglasses with me hiding a French twist under my own hat and dark specs in case I ran into anyone who knew me.

Later, we explored Legacy Park before wandering through Malibu Country Mart which is an outdoor plaza including art galleries and stores with handmade crafts from all over the world. We happened upon an organic café in time for lunch.

It was fun to be so casual, enjoying the day without fear of being discovered and without a bodyguard trailing behind. We felt like a normal couple, exploring Malibu and then strolling back home along the beach.

On Monday, I had a long lunch with three close friends I'd worked with. While I was gone, Ki settled in on the deck to write. When my friends asked where I was staying, I realized I'd met my first test. I practiced, "I'm visiting Bree and staying with her in Silver Lake." (Hurdle number one, cleared.)

Of course, my friends wanted to know what it was like living in Seoul and was I dating. I told them the pros and cons of life there. About dating - I'm not very good at lying well when I feel strongly about a topic.

For hurdle number two, I said, "I'm dating a very kind man that I like and we're just getting to know each other." At least the first part of that statement was true.

Judy grinned, "Ok girl, we want more! What's he look like? What does he do? Any potential for things to get serious in Seoul?"

All three were looking at me with keen interest. I didn't like having to lie, but I had to protect my relationship and Ki. Even good friends can have trouble keeping secrets.

I said, "He's tall, handsome, and Korean. He's a manager and music producer that I did some business with. We've had a few dates, as I mentioned. I'm not sure where it's going. I do like him, though. How about each of you? Sonya, what's happening in your love life?"

That handled hurdle number three. Sonya launched a non-stop comedic chronicle of her recent breakup. They each gave me personal updates and got me up to speed on our other friends. It was fun spending time with them again.

I got back to Malibu about five o'clock. When I walked out to the deck where Ki was sitting, he pulled me onto his lap for a serious kiss. "I'm happy with the writing I've accomplished today, under the blue, sunny skies with the powerful waves rolling in.

"I'm feeling so relaxed here, being in nature. I feel freer, more creative and the lyrics are flowing like waves across my mind. I really love this place. I love being here with you."

I answered, "I'm so happy that being here helps you to be more productive. I love it, too, no question."

He told me what I'd hoped to hear, "I think we should come back every winter for a week or even two. If I'm productive while here, Hyun-Tae will be okay with it."

"Ki, that would be wonderful!"

Later, we ordered pizza and salads and watched a movie. We finally saw the American classic, Butch Cassidy and the Sundance Kid. Ki loved it. I'd forgotten it was such a tragicomedy. We laughed through so many scenes and felt touched by the relationship the three main characters had with each other.

Sandy N. Olson

♥

On Tuesday morning, the sky was cloudy, so we drove to the Getty Museum and Gardens a few miles away. It's on a hilltop and on this particular morning, the building was floating in a foggy mist, ethereal. Ki loved the property at first sight, its design, modernist architecture and stunning gardens.

Van Gogh's painting, Irises, is there. We were both transported by the rich blue-green in the leaves and stalks of the flowers. We discussed how he captured the way they were tangled and twisted by the wind into complex shapes.

The flowers themselves were more blue than purple and one of the irises was white, a stand-out from the rest, like Van Gogh himself. He had created this painting while at the asylum where his brother, Theo, had taken him for rest and professional help after Vincent had mutilated his own ear during a deep depression.

The beautiful painting of the irises was one he did on the grounds of the hospital. We both felt moved by the truism that something so beautiful can result from life's saddest events. The audio tour gave us details about each work as we walked through the large rooms.

Ki loved to be informed about every painting and sculpture. We shared our stand-out pieces with each other and the reasons we loved them. Ki had an in-depth awareness of the artistic choices the painter made in many works.

It was a pleasure listening to his comments. Also, he was interested in what it was about my favorites that pulled me in. Several hours passed as we explored, feeling inspired by the creativity surrounding us from gallery to gardens.

After the museum, we got sandwiches and tea from an outdoor café on the grounds, then continued to the Getty gardens. By then, the morning fog and mist had cleared away and the sun was shining on the extraordinary flowers and cacti. We sat on a bench, read about and discussed the plants we were seeing.

That evening, we had dinner in the Getty's upscale restaurant with sweeping views of LA and the coastline in the distance. The meal was super fresh and delicious.

As we talked about the paintings we had seen, I told Ki about a class I had in college, "It was a large art appreciation class that I took as an elective during a quarter when I had more homework than I could manage. There must have been over one-hundred students in the class. The professor didn't take attendance and I skipped the class anytime I was too busy with other work.

"The final grade was based on one essay we would each write about a painting in a nearby museum. The professor told us our essay had to be about what we appreciated seeing in one of ten paintings in a particular gallery in the museum. He explained that none of the paintings was famous enough to be discussed online, so we wouldn't be able to find info there."

Ki said, "Sounds like an interesting assignment."

I replied, "It was. But at that time, I confess I knew very little about art. So, I didn't feel very confident. All members of the class had a couple weeks to visit the museum at whatever hour they chose. The day I went, very few people were in the room. I selected a painting and sat down on a bench in front of it, jotting down a few notes. I didn't have much to say.

"Soon, a woman began leading a tour of about eight people through the room and arrived at the painting I had chosen. She began explaining what made it special. I tapped *record* on my phone for a voice memo and captured her detailed descriptions. Then, went back to the dorm and typed my paper, adding my own observations to hers. Even then, I had only six pages and was concerned my essay wasn't long enough. But I turned it in during the next class."

Ki said, "Did you get into trouble?"

"That's the funniest part. When we went to the class after the papers were graded, the professor said that the top grade went to an essay that was only six pages long but was exacting and to the point with excellent descriptions of the painting. As he started reading a few excerpts I realized it was my paper! I got an A in the class. I felt a little guilty but very happy."

We both laughed. Ki said, "You were a clever but naughty girl." He gave me a kiss on the cheek. "I like that story and your choice to respect the assignment and your professor by not letting him down."

I guess our waiter, his name tag read Bill, could see that we were happy and in love with each other as we talked non-stop. He brought us complimentary glasses of wine and desserts of apple pie and ice cream. Because we were speaking in Korean some of the time, he asked if we were on vacation in the US. Ki said, "Yes."

Bill responded, "That's why I brought you an all-American dessert." He made us feel so welcome. Of course, Ki tipped him generously. By the time we got up to leave, it was ten p.m. and the restaurant was ready to close. To my surprise, Bill gave me the beautiful flower arrangement and vase that was at the front of the room. I was delighted, how sweet. The bouquet brightened our vacation house.

I've noticed that being happy and loving is contagious. Other people enjoy being part of it, even in a small way. It was thrilling to feel that Ki and I could have that effect. I thought about how it was similar to the way he affects his fans. Stardom, especially the way I see Ki use it, can really be a gift in the world.

When we got home, we sat in the hot tub again, with the stars twinkling above us and the waves rolling in. It was mesmerizing. We talked about the exquisite Getty paintings and gardens. Then we showered together in candle light and got into the big comfy bed. Ki was lying on his stomach, propped up on his elbows. He kissed me and said, "Would you enjoy making love again tonight?"

I smiled and put my hand on his cheek, "I would love it."

He made me feel wonderful. Another perfect finish to a beautiful day.

♥

On Wednesday, we left for our short flight to San Francisco to visit my mom and brother. Ki got "Roberto" out of the beard box and managed to do some more writing on the plane.

Since I was in total vacation mode, I looked through some American celebrity magazines that I hadn't seen while in Korea. We landed a couple hours later and rented a car for the drive to my mom's house where we were staying during this visit instead of my brother's place. When we drove into her driveway, she came out to greet us.

As she gave me a big hug, she said, "I'm so happy to see you two again."

As she hugged Ki, she said, "Ki, you look so different with a beard and mustache. It's quite becoming."

Ki smiled, "I'll tell you a secret. It's fake. I wore it as a disguise in case there might be fans on the plane." Mom was surprised and said, "I never would have guessed that it's not real."

We had eaten breakfast but it was close to noon by the time we arrived. Mom had made a lunch for us. When we planned our trip, I'd reminded my family that we have to keep our visit a secret. They knew from our discussions at Thanksgiving that they couldn't tell anyone about my relationship with Ki.

Mom's house has rows of twelve-foot-tall oleander trees lining each side of her property. Once we had driven into the driveway, the neighbors on either side couldn't see us. But mom has a lady living on one side who can be quite nosy. Just as we were sitting down for lunch in the dining room, we could see her coming up the walk carrying a plate of something.

Mom said, "Oh, no. Here comes nosy Nora. She's wanting to know who's here. I'll get rid of her. She's not getting passed the door."

Mom went to the door in the living room and we could hear Nora saying she brought some of her homemade chocolate chip cookies that were fresh out of the oven. Mom said, "That's lovely, Nora. Thank you. I would invite you in but I need to talk privately with my guests. We're preparing my will."

Nora said, "Oh my goodness, I don't want to interfere." And off she went.

Mom came back to the table and winked at us, "Nora is terrified of dying. She hasn't made a will. I knew if I mentioned any discussion of it, she would run away as quickly as possible. She does make delicious cookies though." She laughed.

We laughed too. Ki said, "I see where Mara gets her excellent negotiating skills."

"Yes, Mom is very clever about managing people. She could always talk Dan and me into doing housework or homework when she wanted us to."

Then I looked at mom and said, "Thank you, Mom, you set a good example for us and raised two hard workers. We love you – and Dad – for being such excellent role models."

About 5 p.m., Dan and Selena arrived with Teddy and Janie in tow. We all hugged. Selena brought some of her delicious homemade recipes. We had an evening of good talk, food and fun together. I felt so "at home" being with my family and Ki as we talked. Ki fit right in and told me later that he feels very comfortable being part of my family. He thoroughly enjoyed the night.

The next day, we left the children with a babysitter. Dan, Selena, Mom, Ki and I piled into the SUV we'd rented and drove to San Francisco. We walked around Fisherman's Wharf where we had lunch, including the classic tourist clam chowder in hollowed-out bowls made of freshly baked sourdough bread.

Then, we drove across the Golden Gate Bridge to Muir Woods where there is a forest of giant sequoia trees, also known as redwoods. They are over 200 feet tall and some are more than eight hundred years old. Ki had never been there. He was awed beneath these trees in the haunted mist of the mountain's interior woods. We all were, even though my family had been to Muir Woods many times.

After a few hours hiking, we drove to Sausalito where we had reservations in a private room on the second floor of one of the better restaurants. The room had large windows affording us a view of the Golden Gate Bridge, San Francisco across the bay and the charming village street below. As the sun was setting, the lights came on in the city and along the bridge, making our view even more spectacular. I loved looking over to see that Ki was entranced.

We were all telling funny stories. I told my family how because of Ki's beard and mustache, I called him Roberto on the plane and pretended I had just met him.

I confessed, "I was whispering in his ear, 'Wow, you're so hot, Roberto.'" Even mom was cracking up. Ki closed with, "As long as she doesn't want me to wear it to bed, I can laugh about it." That was the funniest comment of all.

As we were eating and talking, Ki slipped his credit card to the waiter without my family noticing, covering the cost of the meal that night. Dan later offered to chip in but Ki just shook his head.

We dropped Dan and Selena at their house and got to Mom's about eleven. We were tired. Ki took a quick shower, giving Mom and me a few minutes to talk.

She said, "Mara, it's wonderful to see you and Ki so happy together."

I smiled, "I'm very happy, Mom, I finally found my prince." She responded, "He is truly that."

The next morning, after breakfast, we took a walk with mom around her big backyard. She had lots of flowers growing, a couple of fruit trees, fig and Santa Rosa plum, and a garden of winter vegetables.

Ki was impressed with what she had accomplished with only the help of a local gardener, when needed.

He said, "I'd like to have a yard and garden someday. I hope I can retire early and devote most of my time to making this kind of home for our family, maybe here in California."

Mom said, "I hope you can too, Ki. This is a lovely way to live. I don't know how you and the boys work so hard. I've heard you say in interviews how the band practices twelve hours a day on the choreography. The results are amazing! I can understand why BL6 has become so famous. But I don't know how you have the strength for it."

Ki smiled, "Thank you, Jane. I appreciate your kind words. We do eat well and do a lot of Pilates to stay strong." He put his arm around my mom as we walked to the house.

Mom wanted to show Ki the downtown area of the village she lived in. We drove around the tree-lined streets with old-fashioned lampposts and baskets of living bouquets on each block.

A bookstore there featured both rare and used titles. Ki wanted to see if they had an American book that he had been looking for but couldn't find online. Mom and I explored a sculpture gallery next door. After fifteen minutes, he dashed into the gallery and told us that he had found the book.

He was thrilled, "I've been looking for this book for a year. I can't believe it was hiding in this little shop." He then became interested in the sculptures and bought a small one for our condo to commemorate our trip. He had never lived in a small town but thought he might enjoy the pace and familiarity in the future.

We had lunch in mom's favorite restaurant on the village square. Ki had worn his disguise. No one bothered us, although a young woman at a nearby table kept looking at him off and on as though she might recognize him but wasn't sure. Then, again, maybe she was looking because he was the most handsome man in the room.

About 3:00, it was time to gather our things and kiss Mom goodbye. We stopped at Dan and Selena's to see the kids and say goodbye to them before heading to the airport.

While there, Dan showed us how he was remodeling the bathroom and guest bedroom. They were knee deep in color swatches. Selena showed us beautiful fabric she'd chosen for the drapes. It was a perfect close for our small-town visit. We gave the kids some gifts we'd found in Mom's little village and everyone hugged as we said goodbye.

On the long trip back to Seoul, Ki did more writing. This time, I wrote too, journaling about the whole visit like a literary souvenir. Plus, I had a novel to read that San-A from Social was begging me to finish while I had "so much down time." But we slept during most of the thirteen-hour flight. Because we were in first class, we had comfortable, wide seats that reclined all the way, kind of irresistible.

When we landed in Seoul, we exited separately from the plane. So often there were paparazzi waiting for celebrity photos. We even took separate cabs home because the photogs were outside. We each had put on a medical mask, sunglasses and bucket hats to cover most of our face and hair. People at the airport weren't expecting to see Ki and he made it to a cab without fanfare.

Ki had a new perspective after this trip. He was determined to have more relaxation in his life.

He talked with the guys in the band to see how they enjoyed their time away. They loved it and each had made good songwriting progress. They came back inspired and believed that having a working vacation a couple of times a year would be productive. Hyun-Tae was pleased with the material they had developed and agreed. It was a start toward a more balanced life.

12 *The Unexpected*

It was a month later, when Ki and I were with friends at a restaurant, that a Korean tabloid photographer snapped a photo of us. In the photo, as we were leaving the private room where we'd dined, Ki was beside me, leaning toward me to say something in my ear.

The photo and headline appeared in the news the next day in the same tabloid that offered BestStars a chance to kill the story before. Headline font read: "Is BL6's Lee Ki-Yoon Dating this Blonde American? Looks Like It!" The story was short, telling where the photo was taken and who we were with. But they didn't know my name.

Ki and some of our friends got twitter questions from reporters asking who I am. For this very reason, I'd never opened anything but Finstas for social media – no twitter, Instagram, or Facebook accounts in my own name. I'd always been spotlight-shy but, once I was in the PR industry, I never wanted reporters to link me to any of my firm's clients.

Everyone in our group of diners agreed when BestStars asked them to say that I was a friend of one of the women in the group and that Ki was not dating me. Of course, that info was not published. As with my story to my LA friends, both statements were true since Ki and I were well beyond dating.

As a result of the photo and headline, Ki received hateful tweets from extreme fans who didn't want him dating anyone, especially an American. Some of the comments from true sasaengs were vicious, calling both of us despicable names. There were even threats to kill us.

Ki didn't read his twitter feed for a few weeks. One of the staff members took care of it, avoiding answers to the hateful comments, but answering fans who had positive things to say since most fans sent 'best wishes' to him. The experience was scary for me, especially knowing that Ki received death threats against us. But our security manager didn't believe they were serious enough to be concerned.

Also, I didn't want our relationship to hurt Ki's popularity. But he assured me that nothing was more important than the two of us being together and that the reactions to the story would fade away soon.

Even so, that afternoon, I ordered black hair dye and after delivery, covered my hair. As I waited for it to take effect, I felt the fear of knowing that some people actually wanted to kill us because we loved each other. That was a terrifying thought. Sadness swept over me and tears filled my eyes thinking we were hated because of our beautiful romance.

Many paparazzi knew what condo building we lived in; for about a week, a group of them were waiting outside, cameras ready, evidently waiting for a blonde American to appear. They weren't allowed in the gated parking area.

When I needed to go somewhere, I got into a chauffeur-driven car with tinted windows inside the parking deck. I wore dark glasses. The paparazzi never found me.

Eventually, the discussion died down as Ki said it would. But we knew the day would come when the truth about us would be revealed.

Ki teased me about having black hair. He called me 'Roberta' and told me how hot *I* was.

♥

One night, a few weeks later, Ki and I returned after an evening at a friend's home. As we came off the elevator, a beautiful young Korean woman was sitting on the floor by our condo door.

When she saw us, she ran to Ki and flung her arms around his neck, hugging him. She said, "I know you love only me. You told me that."

Ki removed her arms from his neck and pushed her away. He said, "Jiwon, stop it. How did you get in here?"

I was stunned. I looked at Ki and said, "You know this woman?"

Jiwon then looked at me and was full of rage as she spoke in the most hateful tone I've ever heard - it was a hissing growl.

"Ki doesn't love you. He's been seeing me and making love to me ever since you arrived. He can't give me up!" She grinned in a menacing way. "We have a child together. He'll soon drop you and I'll be living here with him and our son."

Ki had taken out his phone and called the police but before he could speak, Jiwon pulled a knife from her purse and raised it toward me. This happened in seconds. I backed away until I was against the wall. She snarled, "Now, I'm going to kill you."

Ki dropped the phone and lunged at her just as her hand, gripping the knife, plunged downward. He grabbed her arm, wrestling the knife away but slicing the palm of his left hand in the process.

I ran to the phone and was shaking as I picked it up, "There's a woman trying to kill us, please come to 522 Hannam The Hill. Please hurry, she has a knife and has stabbed my fiancé."

The policewoman said, "Police are on their way. Who am I speaking with?"

"Mara Jansen. We'll also need a paramedic. My fiancé's hand is cut and bleeding badly."

Jiwon ran to the staircase door, pushed it opened and disappeared. The bloody knife was on the floor. I told the police, "She just went into the stairwell. Her name is Jiwon. Ki, what is her family name?"

Ki said, "Lee."

"Her family name is Lee." Hearing that her last name was the same as Ki's, tears welled up in my eyes and overflowed. My whole body was now shaking. I thought, *is she telling the truth?*

Ki put his arm around me, holding his other arm and bleeding hand upward.

The policewoman on the phone said, "Ms. Jansen, the police are at the building. They caught her coming out of the staircase door. An officer and a paramedic will be at your condo in minutes."

I was crying now. "Thank you," I whispered.

As he held me, Ki said, "I'm so sorry, Mara, I'm so sorry."

Through my sobs, I asked, "Ki, who is she to you? What is this about?"

Just then, the officer and paramedic exited the elevator. Ki let go of me and unlocked our door. The medic immediately pressed a sterile ice pack against his palm to stop the bleeding.

We all went inside to the kitchen where the medic washed Ki's wound, swabbed it with a numbing antiseptic gel, stitched it closed and bandaged it. With her help, he removed his jacket. His shirt sleeve was bloody. He had another cut, a small one, on his arm which the medic swabbed and bandaged. She then put a cast on his hand so that he couldn't move it and accidentally pull the stitches loose.

The officer asked if we knew Lee Jiwon.

Wiping my tears away and trying to calm down, I heard Ki say, "I knew her for a short time a few years ago."

I suddenly felt sick. "Excuse me." I ran to the bathroom, shut the door and threw up into the toilet.

Ki came into the room. He helped me to my feet, holding me against him. I laid my head on his chest.

He said, "Mara, please look at me." With tears in his eyes, he searched mine. "Nothing she said is true. Nothing." He then held me close to him. "I'm so sorry you had to go through this."

I wrapped my arms around his waist, "Why did she come here? Why did she say all of that? She tried to kill me!"

Ki said, "She's mentally ill. Let's go talk to the police so I can explain to them and to you at the same time."

He went back to the kitchen while I brushed my teeth and rinsed my mouth, then made my way back. The medic had gone but a second officer had now arrived. Ki had gotten a beer from the fridge and offered the officers one. They declined, being on duty, but each took a soda. I poured myself a glass of wine and suggested we all sit down in the living room. Ki and I sat on the sofa, the officers in chairs facing us, ready to take notes.

Ki began, "I haven't seen or heard from this woman for about five years. At that time, I dated her for a short while, maybe four or five dates during one month. I was 19 then. She developed a delusional attachment to me and I ended the relationship. Later, I heard that she had moved into an asylum for professional help."

The policeman asked, "Why do you think she came here after all this time."

Ki replied, "It could be because there was a photo of me and Mara, my fiancé, on a gossip site and newsstands this week. Maybe it triggered something in her mind."

One policeman got a call at that point and said a few words. When it ended, he said, "We've verified that Lee Jiwon was in the Korean Institute for Mental Health for three and a half years but was recently released to a half-way house. Do you want to press charges? It sounds as though it's a clear case of attempted murder of the two of you. We'll keep the bloody knife as evidence."

Thinking as a publicity manager, I asked, "Does that mean we would have to go to court and the story would reach the press?"

The policeman said, "That's debatable. Because the suspect is mentally disturbed, you may be able to go before a judge in a closed court. He could hear the case and return her to a secure mental facility. I suggest that you get a lawyer if you want that to happen. I imagine she could receive a significant sentence. I understand she is from a well-off family and that they have been raising her child. Are you the father of that child, sir?"

I felt sick again and Ki looked shocked, "I didn't know she had a child. I don't believe it's mine."

"The child is about four years old. His full name matches yours - Lee Ki-Yoon."

Ki looked at me and said, "I knew nothing about this."

My mind was reeling. I began to feel numb. *Could the love of my life whom I've trusted with my whole heart, with everything I am, be the father of a crazy woman's son. I can't stand the thought of it. Why didn't he tell me about this woman? He should have. I was filled with confusion, anger and sadness.*

The police said they would investigate further. They explained that Jiwon would be placed in lockdown in a mental ward later tonight. They gave Ki their cards and left.

He looked at me. "I'm so sorry, Mara." He held me in his arms for a few minutes. I was too confused to speak. Ki said, "I should phone Hyun-Tae and tell him what's happened."

"Yes, of course," I replied from a state of numbness. "I'm going into the bedroom while you do that."

I removed my clothes, put on pajamas and got into bed. Under the blankets, I curled up into a ball. But my mind wouldn't relax. I googled how long it takes to get paternity test results - one to two days. I wondered if her parents knew the month that she became pregnant. It seemed that if they thought the child was Ki's, they would have contacted him for support, knowing he's wealthy. *I have to try to stay calm.*

Ki came into the room. He took off his shoes and got into his side of the bed. He said, "May I hold you?"

I leaned into him. He wrapped his arms around me. I said, "Ki, why didn't you tell me about her?"
"It was so long ago that I didn't even think of her. I haven't thought about her in years."

"Can that child be yours? I mean, did you wear condoms when you were nineteen?"

"Sometimes. Not all the time. That was the dark period I went through, acting out. I was at such a low point, emotionally. I was reckless, didn't care whether I lived or died."

I said, "I feel sick all over, every part of my body. I can't stand thinking about this. I'm so sad and angry. I felt safe here with you and now that feeling has been shattered into a million pieces. I don't know if I'll ever feel safe here again. How are you feeling? How's your hand?"

He said, "I'm drained emotionally. My hand feels okay, the numbing gel on my palm worked. Also, Hyun-Tae said we're probably both in shock. He's sending a prescription medication over that will calm us. Would you like to try that?"

"Normally, I wouldn't, but, yes. I think I need something. My mind and nerves are wrecked."

Within a few minutes, Ki got a call from the lobby about the delivery. He said, "Please have security bring it up." He went to the door, then returned with a glass of water and a small pill for me. He took two of them, got back in bed and held me.

Within about twenty minutes I felt less pain, my nervous system began relaxing and my whole body started feeling better. I said, "That works fast. What else did Hyun-Tae say?"

"He said that he'll get me the number of a good criminal lawyer."

I said, "How did she get up here? How did she even know which condo we live in?"

"I don't know. The police are going to investigate that."

"Ki, you saved my life. That knife was headed for my heart. I was against the wall and couldn't move. It was happening in seconds."

"But it happened because of me. I'm sorry that you had to experience it. I love you so much. I never wanted to cause you pain or fear of any kind."

I could hear the overwhelming emotions in his voice, I looked at him, "Ki, what happened was Jiwon's responsibility, not yours. You couldn't know that she would do something like this."

Soon, we both started feeling drowsy because of the drug. We fell asleep in each other's arms.

♥

The next morning, I woke up about ten, hours later than usual. The drug really knocked me out. But the horrible events of last night came thundering back to mind, crushing my heart like a boulder. My chest felt physically painful. Ki was already up. I could hear his voice from the desk in his office, talking with someone on his cell.

I got up, took a shower and shampooed my hair, trying to wash some of the sadness away. Then I got dressed and went to the kitchen for some orange juice as I started the coffee.

When Ki came in, he held me close and kissed me, saying, "How are you feeling this morning?"

"Sad," I answered. "Probably less in shock, more accepting that it happened and we're both still alive, thank God." I got mugs from the cupboard. "Did you eat breakfast?"

"Yes, I don't need anything, thanks. I just talked with the police. We have a detective heading the case. He told me that he spoke with Jiwon's parents. They were very upset when they learned what happened. They don't know who the father of the boy is. They love him and are enjoying raising him. They want time to think about whether to have the paternity test."

I asked, "What's the next step?"

His eyes looked sad as he spoke, "I feel that I have to find out if the boy is my son."

I took in a long breath, "I knew you would feel that way. I do, too. And, if he is your son, what will you do?"

Ki slowly shook his head as though forming the next words was almost too difficult, "I wouldn't want him to grow up thinking that his dad doesn't care about him. That's a heavy burden for a child to carry. I feel that I would have to be in his life to some extent. I'm concerned about how that change, if it happens, will affect you...and our relationship."

"I don't know the answer to that right now. I'm too confused by all of this. Let's wait until we learn the truth."

At that point, Ki's phone rang. It was Hyun-Tae suggesting an attorney and giving Ki his number. He asked how we were doing this morning. Ki said, "Still emotionally overwhelmed for the most part. But thanks for the prescription. It definitely helped us relax and sleep."

Hyun-Tae said, "Call me if there's anything else I can do." Ki reassured him he would and thanked him for his concern before ending the call.

He looked at me, "I should call the attorney. I can go to my office if you want, so you don't have to hear the conversation. We may have to visit him today if he has an opening or maybe he won't require that. Do you have anything already scheduled today?"

"Oh, I hadn't even thought about my schedule. I have one meeting this afternoon but I'm going to cancel it. I can't talk business today. But I can go to see the attorney if we need to, though I'd rather that you take care of it by phone."

Ki went to his office and phoned the lawyer, Park Min-Woo, who said that he would gather information from the detective in charge and that he believed he could get a private hearing with a judge so we can keep it out of the news. He said it looks like an open and shut case. Ki asked him about trying to arrange a paternity test with the grandparents. He agreed.

Ki came back to the kitchen and shared the information, then said, "What would you like to do today? What might free your mind of this for a while?"

I thought for a few minutes, "Since it's winter and we can't go to a park, which I know would help, how about watching the documentary we've wanted to see about hummingbirds? We can make popcorn and a Greek salad. Later we can order whatever we want for dinner."

Ki said, "That sounds good. Do you think you'll tell your family what's happening?"

Tears filled my eyes, "No, they would worry about us. I don't want them to feel the pain that we're feeling. I'll probably never tell them. I may tell Bree though. I won't be able to keep it from her. When something isn't right with me, she knows."

Ki said, "I agree. But, if it turns out that the boy is my son, we'll have to discuss it with both of our families. That's going to be difficult."

"True, but I can't even think about that right now."

It was already close to noon, so I made the Greek salad. Ki made two big bowls of popcorn with butter for me and curry powder for him. We each drank a lemonade as we settled in for the two-hour Netflix documentary. It was captivating, the hummingbirds were beautiful and held our interest, definitely an aid in calming our minds.

As the credits rolled at the end, we heard someone talking outside our door. We had a camera that allowed us to see the hallway and speak to anyone there. From the remote, Ki could see that one of the men was a member of building maintenance. Through the speaker, he asked what was happening. A janitor answered, "We're cleaning the blood from the carpet and wall."

Ki said, "Okay, thank you."

That snapped us back to reality! At least we'd had a couple hours of beautiful birds, flowers and music to enjoy before the weight of it returned. Still, we agreed it was good to keep finding windows of joy before our minds flood again with the sad events that are happening.

I told Ki, "Maybe I'll phone Bree now and see if she has any good advice for me. She's almost like a counselor." I didn't want to leave him with his worries. "Is there something else that you would like to do for emotional relief?"

He said, "I think I'll try to put my feelings into lyrics. That's how I escape when I'm upset."

"Okay. I'm going into the bedroom." We stood up and hugged each other for several seconds. I kissed him and said, "I love you."

He managed a smile, "I love you, too."

> Bree, are you at home or in public?

> Home. Solo. You ok?

> Can I please call you?

13 *Mara's Escape*

As soon as she said 'Hello,' I started crying. "Bree, something terrible has happened."

"Mara, what on earth is it? It must be terrible if you're crying. Is Ki all right?"

"I'm sorry to burden you but I need your guidance. Yes, Ki is okay. But a mentally ill fan, a woman Ki dated four years ago, tried to kill us last night."

"Oh, my God, Mara! How did it happen?"

I went on to tell her the details including the child that could be Ki's. I was sobbing as I talked.

She said, "This is really shocking!"

"Yes, it is. I haven't told Ki this and I feel guilty thinking it, but I'm wondering if I want to live this life, this life of secrecy and constant threats."

I went on to tell Bree, "Ki and the other band members get regular death threats and the security team tries to determine whether they're serious. How can I raise our children in this kind of atmosphere? If this crazy woman found where we live, anyone could."

Bree said, "I can understand your feelings after what you went through. I think it's completely normal to question whether you want to live with this kind of threat. But I do think that this is an aberration. It's very rare that someone tries to act on their threats. Very few celebrities have been injured or killed by a crazy fan or by anyone."

I replied, "Yes, I know that's true. I keep reminding myself. The other question is - if the boy this woman had is Ki's, would I want to help raise the child of the woman who tried to kill me?! Ki and I had such a beautiful life together and now… it's so complicated."

Bree said, "Mara, in this situation, you have to take one step at a time." I took a breath and focused on her voice, "If the boy is Ki's, it could be that you'll both fall in love with him and he'll be a joy. For now, keep every positive possibility in mind."

I began to cry again, "I'm so confused right now with these shocking changes. I knew about the threats and about what's happened to other idols but I admit I tried not to think about them. And I never imagined that Ki could have a child out there in the world, actually, living right here in Seoul.

"He'd told me a while back that he went through a dark phase emotionally. That's when he dated this woman for a month before realizing she was sick. She's very beautiful. I can see why any man would be attracted to her."

Bree suggested, "How about coming to California for a week or so to get your mind off everything? It could be good to have a break."

As always, she said what I was thinking, "I thought about it but I would feel guilty leaving Ki alone during this. It's very difficult for him as well."

Bree responded, "Mara, it's really *his* situation to deal with, not yours. It's his past that showed up to try to kill you. You're allowed to take a break. It's sunny and warm here. We could go to all our favorite places. You deserve a chance to relax."

I mulled it over for a few seconds, "You have a point, this happened because of his choices in the past. Maybe I should put my own needs first right now."

Bree could tell I was seeing more clearly, "I would love to see you and hang out. We could have some fun together in spite of everything."

"Thank you, Bree! Let me think it through for a while and text you later tonight. Oh, by the way, what's happening in your life...hopefully beautiful events?"

We talked another thirty minutes or so before ending our call. It was a help to hear her voice. I went to Ki's office. He was still writing. I asked, "How's it going?"

"It's helping me get my emotions out. So that's good. It's been a powerful session. How was your talk with Bree?" He sounded calmer, steadier than this morning.

"It was helpful, too. She invited me to take a break and get some sun by visiting her." I could see his concern even though he tried to cover it, but I continued, "I feel as though I need to take a few days, care for myself. Is there anyone you would want to come over?"

"Bin would come over. I feel okay talking with him. You and I could FaceTime each day. That is, if you want to."

"Of course, I want to." I sat down on his lap and put my arms around him. "I love you and, right now, want to take care of you emotionally. But part of me is so sad and so terrified that I really want to run away from this building, from the hallway where I was almost killed and the news that you have a son. It's all so burdensome and a few days away will help me."

"*Might* have a son," he corrected, gently. "I understand. Yes, you should visit Bree. Knowing we can FaceTime, Bin's visits, the attorney, Hyun-Tae's advice and more writing, maybe a lot more…I'll probably manage." He smiled when he saw I got his humor, "I'll miss you but I think I can survive." He caressed my cheek, "But please, Mara, please come back to me."

"I will, sweetheart. I love you." We held each other for a few moments. Way in the back of my mind, I wondered if I *could* come back. It's one thing to read or even know first-hand about someone's life being threatened; it's another thing to live through it. It's terrifying and extremely sad. You realize that feeling safe is just an illusion.

Later, I booked a flight to LA for the next evening and texted Bree.

> Bree, thank you for the talk. Just thank you. See you Sat., 3pm curbside, Int'l Tmnl, LAX.

> I'll be there. Love you! Hope you 2 can sleep.

That night, Ki and I made love with a tenderness we'd never had before, as if we were reaching for the safety of the innocent love we'd enjoyed since we met.

♥

In the morning, the lawyer called Ki and said the closed court hearing was scheduled for three weeks from now. Also, he had spoken with the grandparents of the boy. They wanted to meet Ki before deciding whether to agree to a paternity test. Ki said to tell them he would do that and for them to choose any day and time within the week.

That evening, I flew to LA and arrived there mid-day. Bree was at the airport to pick me up. It was sunny and warm outside. It was strange how immediately I felt "at home" again. Bree and I talked non-stop on our way to her place. We also stopped at one of our favorite restaurants and picked up veggie burgers, sweet potato fries and salad.

At Bree's house, we sat on her backyard deck, surrounded by the stunning flowers of her Angel's Trumpet and Gold Medallion trees swaying in the warm breeze. It felt wonderful.

At one point she said, "You'll never guess who I talked with the other day."

"Who?"

"Your last boyfriend, James, the attorney. He's been working in Hanoi the last couple of years, started his own business there. He had tried calling you but you've changed phones and I haven't. So, I picked up. He's in LA this week. I didn't tell him you would be here."

I laughed, "Oh, my gosh, what a coincidence after all this time."

"He would love to talk with you. Maybe you should give him a call for the fun of it. Probably no one's threatening *his* life."
"That's true. It's unusual that the two men I've been involved with most recently both live in Asia."

Bree and I talked through the afternoon and early evening until Ki FaceTimed. He told me that Bin came over and spent part of the day. The weather was a little warmer, a whopping 5°C (41°F for us Americans) and they drove out to the country in Bin's new sports car.

He said, "Bin always makes me laugh and yesterday was non-stop jokes. Being with him helped. We had dinner in a little restaurant with food that tasted homemade. It was delicious."

Ki didn't tell me that the meeting with the boy's grandparents was scheduled this week and I didn't ask. I talked about the weather and Bree's beautiful backyard. I didn't mention that James was in LA and wanted to see me.

In the morning Bree and I went out to the beach for a walk in the sun and to watch the waves roll in. We took beach towels for after the walk and had what the shop owner called "breakfast wine" with the picnic brunch she had packed.

God, I've missed this - soaking up some rays in our shorts and halter tops. It was good sitting next to Bree, to be with my bestie, letting her manage the details. Really, it was a perfect California day.

14 *Realization*

Back home from the beach, Bree asked, "Are you going to tell Dan and your mom about this?"

"No, I don't want them to worry."

"Wow. Mara, you've always been so close to them. Now part of your life is going to be secret? I don't want to pull a reversal here but that's extreme. To live with Ki and hide part of who you are from your own family. That's not you. That's not healthy emotionally."

"I know. That aspect of it makes me more confused."

Being on the beach brought back the memory of lunch with Ki in Santa Monica. It was our third date. I thought about how innocent it was, just having him touch my hand was exciting. How distant all of it seemed now. So much can happen between two people in under a year.

Bree had a professional dinner engagement that evening. While she got ready, I sat at her kitchen table in silence. The idea of being alone was bleak. Instantaneously, my hand reached for my phone.

> Dinner at 8? Let me know where. M

> Mara? You're in town. Absolutely! I'll pick you up. Bree's at 7?

There was no way I could spend the night alone in Bree's house with the thoughts I was thinking.

I texted Ki to let him know that Bree and I were both going out with some friends that evening. But we'd still FaceTime later. I didn't tell him the whole truth because I was mainly going for the company. No need to worry him.

James picked me up at seven. When I opened Bree's front door, he said, "My God, Mara, you're even more beautiful than I remember."

"Thank you, James. You look great yourself. Hanoi must be good for you."

As we walked to the car, he answered, "Well, it's been good for my bank account. My business has taken off. I have nine Vietnamese employees, all fluent in English. We're doing very well helping American corporations set up businesses in the country. The laws are complex but favorable for foreign companies."

In the restaurant we started with drinks on the patio. There were flower baskets everywhere as well as lighted gardens and trees across the lawn. I said, "This is really lovely. I've never been here before."

James said, "I asked a colleague to name the best restaurant and he texted this one."

We talked about our experiences as Westerners in the two Asian cultures we were learning about and we talked about our work. In fact, James went on for quite a while. I'd forgotten about his habit of talking more than he listened.

He didn't know about K-pop music. But he was intrigued to learn that BL6 had become superstars around the world and he complimented me on having such a high-level job, managing their global touring publicity.

After dessert, he said, "I've missed you, Mara. I think of you often. I've never found anyone to match the person you are – not even close."

"Those are very kind words, James. I know there are a lot of accomplished and beautiful Vietnamese women. I can't imagine that you've escaped romance."

He replied with a smile, "Romance and love are two different things. How about you? Are you involved with anyone?"

It was clear where James was headed. I wanted to tell him the truth. "I'm in love with a South Korean man. We've been together almost a year. He's genuine, handsome, interesting and very considerate." I held up my engagement ring which James either didn't notice or had chosen to ignore.

"Is he successful, Mara, because you deserve the best?"

"Thank you, James. Yes, he's very successful."

We continued talking as he drove me to Bree's and walked me to the door. He said, "Can I text you tomorrow?"

"James, I'm really glad to have talked with you tonight. Thank you for a lovely evening. I wish you happiness in your life, but let's agree to leave this here."

He kindly agreed. We gave each other a hug and parted ways.

After spending an evening with James, the nicest and most successful guy I had ever dated, I knew that, in spite of the danger and secrecy of celebrity life, I had never loved anyone else as much as I do Ki. The dinner with James reminded me, too, no one had ever loved me as much as Ki does.

I got home about 11P.M. and wondered if he was home.

> Still feel like talking?

And seeing your face? Yes

It was a short conversation. All I really wanted was to see him. He didn't have much to say either. It was as though we just needed to sit inside the feeling of love we have for each other. "I'm going to fly back on Friday," I said.

"I'll be waiting. I love you, Mara."

"I love you, too. Goodnight for now."

♥

The encounter with James created some kind of shift for me. I woke up the next day feeling calm, no dreams of Jiwon or the knife – like all of it, even the life-long stabbing nightmare, had vanished.

I didn't want to walk away from Ki the way that couple who'd met one night in Barcelona had walked away from each other. I wasn't willing to sacrifice my time living deeply in love to improbable fears or some false hope that I'd find something equally meaningful again.

Telling Bree at breakfast, we laughed at how a random encounter – those few hours with James – had cleared my mind and our calendar. No more heavy analysis, just beach time. After a couple more days of relaxation with her – my confidant, my safety net – we hugged each other and said goodbye for now.

It was amazing to feel so sure that I was ready, flying back to Seoul.

When I got off the plane about 9 p.m. a waiting chauffeur held a sign with my name on it. Underneath in parentheses, it read, 'Roberto.' I smiled. Ki had written it in his own handwriting to assure me that I was safe.

To avoid reporters, I wore sunglasses, a scarf covering my blonde-again hair and a wide-brimmed hat. The chauffeur led me to a black Mercedes. Arriving at the car, he opened the back door for me. There was Ki, beaming joy with a bouquet of long-stemmed roses and open arms.

I said, "You're *here*!"

He replied, "I am! And, *you're* here!"

I slid into the seat and into his embrace. "I missed you so much! Thank you for the flowers, they're beautiful." I kissed his gorgeous lips.

He had on a tan knit shirt, navy blue jacket and jeans. I continued, "You look so handsome."

The glass partition and curtains separated us from the driver. The side and back windows were tinted for total privacy. Romantic music played softly.

I removed my coat. hat, scarf and asked, "May I sit on your lap? I want to feel your body against me."

Ki said, "Of course, Babe."

I straddled his lap and pressed my body into his. I slid my arms around his waist, moving my hands under his shirt, up his back and around to his chest. He was like oxygen. I couldn't get enough.

He began kissing my neck and unbuttoning my silk blouse. He unfastened the front clasp of my bra and his tongue danced across my nipples. I felt beautiful sensations in every cell, exciting and peaceful at the same time.

He ran his hands up my bare legs, unsnapped my thong, then moved his hand between my legs over the most sensitive area of my body, touching all the right spots. My nerve endings were quivering with exquisite pleasure.

I unbuttoned and unzipped his jeans, the familiar thrill of no underwear – he seldom wore any.

He gently pushed inside me. His hands held my thighs, spreading my legs wider. The next entries were deeper and harder. I drew in a full, quick breath as I held his body to mine. The feelings were overwhelming. We were gasping with each thrust, building to a crescendo.

Then, an explosive orgasm, both of us! We each cried out. Our bodies pulsing as if we had one heart. Everything inside me reacted in blissful harmony – ecstatic! We were showered in joyful sensations. It felt so good, physically, to connect again.

My hands pressed against Ki's back, on his warm skin, holding him tight. My only thought was how much I love him.

We held each other until our breathing relaxed. Then we looked at each other, glowing, and started giggling in sheer delight.

From my haze of happiness, I managed, "Oh my god, that was amazing!"

He said, "Even beyond amazing, it was all consuming! The sensations were so *potent*! We've never had sex with you on my lap. You've never been so assertive before."

"I've never been away from you for a week before."

The car was still speeding down the highway but getting close to home. We got dressed just before entering the parking deck.

With his arms around me, Ki said, "I didn't know what to expect when you came off the plane. What happened between us was beyond my wildest dreams. This is a beautiful reunion, Mara." Then, he laughed, "That was, without question, the best ride home from the airport I've ever had. I'll never forget it."

I said, "Same here. I loved every exciting, exquisite moment."

15 *The Future*

We exited the elevator to our floor. With each step, I pulled my thoughts away from what had happened there ten days ago.

Once we were inside, Ki kept it positive, "I have a bottle of your favorite champagne to welcome you home." He wrapped his arm around my waist, "Shall we toast?"

"Absolutely!" I was happy to celebrate.

He popped the cork, bringing the ice bucket and two elegant crystal flutes to the living room. He said, as though thinking out loud, "This is a very special occasion."

With those tiny bubbles almost overflowing, he raised his glass. "Mara, I've thought so much about us while here without you. Our extraordinary ride home makes me feel humble to be the man you want and continue to love through all of this. Let's drink a toast to our future together."

I raised my glass. "I wouldn't want a future without you. I love you, Ki – completely." The chime of our glasses seemed to fill our hearts. It will sound in my mind for a long time.

We were together again. This time it felt like forever. I laughed to myself when I realized another Kelly Clarkson tune from my early days in LA was playing in my head. This time, her musical nod to Nietzsche's philosophy was playing: "What doesn't kill you makes you stronger!"

As we sipped our champagne, Ki caught me up on the work he had been doing with BL6 and the fun he and Bin had together.

I decided to share everything and let him know that I'd had dinner with James one night. "When James asked if I was involved with anyone, I told him that I was in love with a handsome, exciting and successful South Korean man."

He laughed, "That's what old boyfriends want to hear. I'm sure he was disappointed."

I smiled. "He wished us much happiness. The only reason I got together with him was because Bree had a professional dinner to attend and I didn't want to be alone. He's just a friend from the past that I don't plan on being in touch with again."

Ki said, "Babe, it's completely okay. I understand. I'm glad, so glad, you came back to me after what you went through."

I kissed him and said, "Ki, I'll never love any man as much as I love you. Nor can I imagine anyone loving me in the kind, amazing way that you do."

After our second glass of champagne, I asked the question we had been avoiding, "What did you learn from the boy's grandparents?"

Ki set down his glass to answer, "We all met at my attorney's office. The grandparents said they had looked for photos of me online after Jiwon insisted that I was the boy's father. But they didn't see a resemblance. It was clear that they love this boy dearly.

Their son accompanied them. He's a personable and successful young businessman. He and his wife also love the child."

I asked, "Did they agree to the paternity test?"

He said, "After we talked for an hour or more, they agreed. The boy and I took a paternity test at different times the next day, I never did see him."

Ki put his hand on mine. "Mara, we weren't a match. I'm not his father. But I'm glad to know he'll be well cared for and loved."

I didn't realize I'd been holding my breath until I let out a sigh of relief and let it sink in. "Are you happy about the results or disappointed? I can't tell."

He smiled, "I'm happy, Mara, so relieved! Still, it makes me very aware of how much I want to be a father to our children. I want to slow down the touring sooner rather than later and have a more normal life. Bin feels the same way. How do you feel about that?"

I said, "I'm all for slowing down and I would be happy having children sooner rather than later."

This was a fresh spark of harmony! We talked and dreamed through the evening. After raiding the fridge of each delicious Korean dish Soo-Jung had waiting for us, finally, we fell into bed and slept, soundly.

♥

Within a couple of weeks, we attended the closed court hearing. Jiwon was not there. Ki and I each testified regarding her actions that night. The detective and police on the scene also testified.

Jiwon was given a long sentence for attempted murder, to be served in a mental health facility. Owing to her lifelong history of mental health issues, it's likely that she will remain institutionalized, with slim chances of release. The case was closed and records sealed. There were no tabloid articles or reporting of any kind about it.

Our attorney told us what the police records revealed. After Jiwon saw the gossip rag photo of us online, she had learned we likely lived in Hannam. She drove around the area until she saw paparazzi in front of our building. With money stolen from her parents, she bribed the lobby desk clerk and that's how she found our condo.

The clerk was fired and charges were brought against him. In a separate hearing, he received six months in prison and a 5M won penalty with five-years of probation because his actions lead to Ki's stabbing and my attempted murder. He was legally bound to agree that if he spoke about us or the event, his charges would be increased.

There was comfort in feeling that justice was served and the courts were swift. It made me very aware of our privilege and that things might not have gone that way with so many having far different dealings with the justice system.

Could something like this happen to us again? Yes. Of course, it would be rare, as Bree emphasized to me in LA. Still, BestStars increased BL6 security substantially after the incident. For instance, our favorite airport driver was screened and hired full time by BestStars security. As other key concerns were addressed, I began to feel more comfortable.

♥

Life kept moving forward. In a few weeks, the full album of songs that Ki and his talented 'brothers' began during our January downtime was released. It included Ki's song about the pain and sadness we endured after Jiwon's attack.

"Despair" flew up the charts. It was so full of raw emotion that it hooked fans and won new listeners, soaring to number one in digital sales and on the Billboard 100. We were happy that something good came out of such a terrifying ordeal.

The song didn't reveal the exact details of our experience. It was a poignant anthem to almost losing a loved one to hate-filled violence and the emotions that surround such a tragedy. Ki sang lead on the track, which I learned he and Bin laid down while I was in LA. He sang most of it in English in my honor because of what I went through. I felt so loved by his thoughtfulness.

The authentic anger and the sadness he was feeling came through to listeners. It moved people in the ways that only art can. So many grieving people, from mom's to movements, said they felt heard and helped by this piece. Ki received excellent reviews.

This was the 'next-level' album that moved BL6 into true international superstardom. That shift prompted us to sell the condo for a newer, larger one with three bedrooms - one a guest bedroom and one for Ki's office - in a more secure building.

We no longer had to walk every single day past the spot where I almost died. But we did opt to stay in the Hannam area.

In our new building, all employees were thoroughly investigated before being hired and were very well paid. They signed contracts explaining that if they gave anyone information about a condo resident, they could be fired, charged with breach of the privacy agreement, even arrested if harm resulted from their disclosure.

With the move came the feeling we'd started a fresh chapter in an epic story. For the first time, too, I shared in the potent joy my celebrity clients feel when hundreds of thousands of fans are deeply touched by work borne of an intimate personal experience. I never expected *that* from my PR career; I guess, not even from my proximity to Ki's artistry or fame. It was a powerful time.

Amid this fresh start, Ki gave me an extraordinary card of an abstract painting that evoked a swirling vision of lovers kissing. He'd inscribed his message in English:

> My Beautiful Mara,
>
> Although I write words of love in my lyrics, I realize that I can't find words meaningful enough or strong enough to express how I feel about you… how much I love you and want to make you happy, how often I want to make love with you, how many minutes a day my mind is filled with thoughts and images of you. You are the only woman I've ever loved. You are the sun in my sky, the stars in my soul. You are everything my heart desired and longed for. I'm so grateful to have found you and to feel that you love me in the beautiful way that you do. Thank you for lifting my life to new heights.
>
>   Ki

Sandy N. Olson

♥

It's a letter I will treasure forever and which I share to bring you joy, Dear Reader, as our beautiful love story comes to a close for now.

We're happy. We feel lucky that our paths crossed in this life and we had the courage to begin dating. We love each other as completely and as considerately as we can and look forward to each day of our future together. A year ago, I didn't even know Ki existed. Now, both our lives are completely changed… proof that magic can happen.

Dear Reader,

Thank you! It means so much to me that you went on my tour of K-pop Secret Love.

If you enjoyed my love story, could you please help me spread the thrill of romance?! Your positive review on the book's Amazon page would mean so much.

I hope you'll enjoy sharing your favorite moments or discoveries with other readers as much as I enjoyed writing this first novel of mine.

Thank you, again, for taking this journey. I wish you the joy of love and a happy heart ahead in your life.

All My Best,

Sandy

P.S. Here's the link to my Amazon page –
https://tinyurl.com/lg5870n3

For more K-pop ♥ secrets, come by my website –
http://www.sandynolson.com

Made in the USA
Coppell, TX
01 March 2021

51048329R00134